Area Bird

by

Susan I. Spieth

Reviews and Awards for Gray Girl

"As a 1985 graduate of the prestigious West Point Military Academy, author Susan Spieth retained the indelible mark of becoming a member of the "Long Gray Line." With that lasting impression she now transports readers to an equally memorable experience in this fictional work that juxtaposes men and women in the military, against the longstanding traditions of honor." (US Review of Books; full review at: http://www.theusreview.com/reviews/Gray-Spieth.html#.VGzoYxb7qlJ)

"It's the early 1980s and Cadet Jan Wishart becomes an instrument for change at an institution that wants to remain the same: The United States Military Academy at West Point. A sexual assault is the catalyst for Cadet Wishart pushing against the grain of this patriarchal institution. This fast-paced book is easy and enjoyable to read, yet is smart and heady in its delivery by shining a bright light on the virtues of honor and friendship. This entertaining novel on cadet life illustrates the power and importance of storytelling by documenting a culture of institutional misogyny in hopes that history does not repeat itself." (Winner – Eric Hoffer Award, e-book fiction)

Readers' Praise for Gray Girl

"Wow. This is a really fantastic book with amazing detail that never becomes tedious, just continues to build the realism and tension of the story. There's a lot to admire about the women she writes about, as well as some of the men. There's also much to be disturbed by, because all of it seems very plausible. (LA Kristy)

Having served at West Point as a Military Police, the book served as a memory trip back to those gray stone buildings with it many statue and iconic sites. Every time Susan mentioned those sites, I was transported there with the remembrance of something that had occurred there during my tour of duty. (William Perez)

Great USMA Mystery novel! I read the book in 2 days and I loved the plebe perspective and details about West Point cadets and the Fourth Class System. (Lansing)

This book made me feel like I was at West Point. At times, the fear and anguish inside Jan brought forth emotional of my own trials in life. I could not put it down! (Teri Motley)

This book is definitely the best book I have read in 2014. (Gayle Armstrong)

I never thought I would enjoy a book about the military, but I loved this one. I could not put it down. (Cog Wheel "Ellie")

This well-written novel keeps you guessing. Just when you think you've got it all figured out, you are thrown the proverbial "curve". A highly recommended read! (Barry Grecu)

The novel may be fiction, but some of the situations ring true to my ears. Could not put it down until I finished it. Excellent first novel. (KWIK)

Great character development, an absorbing storyline, surprise twists at the end that I was not expecting - all bundled together in an excellent look at life as a female plebe at West Point. (Cheryl Stout)

This book is full of suspense and full of surprises. It keeps the pages turning and is hard to put down. The author lived through her academy days and no doubt the book is accurate in its depiction of most everything in academy life. (Bill Bolles)

Loved the self-talk of the young woman who is thrust into a male world at such a vulnerable age. The degradation and humiliation she endured was immense. Her struggle to sustain and keep at it were admirable. A very good read. (S. Germaine)

She made the Academy come to life. Her descriptions of the physical plant, and cadet life, brought back memories to us that were there; and I'm sure opened the eyes of those who were not familiar with the USMA, while creating a fictional story that had us glued to our seats. Kudos Susan. (Bob McCloskey)

(Over 190—5 star reviews from readers at: http://www.amazon.com/Gray-Girl-Susan-I-Spieth/product-reviews/1491272813/ref=cm_cr_pr_hist_5?ie=UTF8&filterBy=addFiveStar&showViewpoints=0&sortBy=bySubmissionDateDescending)

Area Bird is a work of fiction. Names, characters, places and incidents either are the product of the author's imagination or used fictitiously. Any resemblance to actual persons, living or dead, or events is purely coincidental.

 ISBN-13: 978-1500929770
ISBN-10: 1500929778
GrayGirl2013@gmail.com

To my late father, Cornelius F. Ives, for making it too damn hard for me to ever quit West Point. I love and miss you.

And to my sweet husband and fabulous children—you know who you are.

Acknowledgements

Once again, it takes a small army. I have to thank my beta readers who provided excellent feedback on content and flow: Bob Spieth, Barb Eimer, Lisa Bruck, Tracy Seymour and Megan Seymour. They did all the heavy lifting. Then there's Christie Stratos of *Proof Positive,* who worked out the technical kinks like spelling, grammar and punctuation. She's been a real pain in the you-know-what. My cover men: Sean Gumm (photographer) and Chris Zarza (cover designer) are worthy of an Oscar or something. And I have to give a shout out to the Mercer Island Writers' group—which is always willing to tell me when something sucks. They're good at that.

AREA BIRD, n. A cadet who is serving punishment by being obliged to walk on the area.
(Glossary of Cadet Slang, Bugle Notes, '81)

ONE

Freedom can require that need to fight and die,
But Amelia's pristine freedom
was her simple love to fly,
From Boston down to St. John's,
then up and across to Shannon town.
God love the little lassie,
cause she held the hammer down.
(from A.E. by Cornelius F. Ives, 1976)

April 3, 1983
0530 hours

She almost didn't see the car go over the cliff. If it hadn't been for the seat belt buckle pressing into her right butt cheek, she would have missed the flying automobile altogether. The protruding safety feature, however, caused a literal "pain in the ass." She rotated her body, knocking her boyfriend off the back seat. Fortunately, he landed on the hump in the middle of the floorboard, which prevented him from becoming completely stuck in the small space between the front and back seats. With his face mushed up against the red vinyl, he asked, "Um, what did I do to deserve that?"

She sat upright rubbing her sore backside. "Sorry," she said, "didn't mean to wake you."

"Oh, waking wasn't the problem. It was the excruciating fall after that."

"You poor baby," she teased.

The sun began peeking over the horizon and a beam of light streamed through the windshield illuminating her face. They had spent the night in his car, parked at the small scenic overlook at the apex of Storm King Highway. They would have preferred a hotel, but everything from Highland Falls to Newburgh had been booked solid due to Plebe-Parent Weekend. It was also the last day of spring leave for the upperclassmen.

"Why don't you join me down here in the ditch? It's kind of cozy."

"No, thanks, I've already had one thing poking me this morning..."

That's when it happened.

They heard a revving engine followed by screaming wheels. Jan turned her head toward the commotion just in time to see a flash of red whizz by. In hindsight, she would remember the car seemed to glide by their parked car before soaring, in slow motion, up and over the low stone wall. The screeching abruptly stopped as the vehicle disappeared from sight.

"Did you just see that?" she screamed.

"I saw something—what was it?"

"It was a car! I think it was a red sports car!"

He jumped up, sitting beside her on the back seat. "No! Can't be."

She opened the back door. They scrambled out of his 1965 Mustang and raced to the front of the car. They stood beside the stone wall, now with a gaping hole separating the scenic overlook from the dramatic drop-off.

Several hundred feet below, smoldering on its side, with wheels still spinning, the red 1982 Chevy Camaro appeared to be resting. Jan thought the car seemed relieved somehow.

"Jesus," her boyfriend whispered.

"Oh, my God!" she replied just as the sun came fully over the horizon. Then she remembered that it was Easter Sunday.

TWO

YEARLING, n. A member of the Third Class; Also, Yuk. (A Glossary of Cadet Slang, Bugle Notes, 1981, p.294)

August 15, 1982
1030 hours

Damn bells.

Mandatory chapel ended in the early 1970s, however the Cadet Chapel bells still awoke cadets on the only day they could sleep in. The incessant ringing every Sunday morning continued to haze Jan Wishart long after plebe year. Only now, in New South Barracks, she was even closer to the huge, annoying alarm clock.

How hard would it be to take a sledgehammer to those things? Thoughts of sabotage circled her brain until she awoke enough to realize that the bells were the least of her worries.

She and her thousand or so classmates had recently returned to West Point at the start of "Re-Orgy" week. Jan felt somewhat relieved that it was pronounced with a hard "g" as in "great" as opposed to a soft "g" as in "general." Short for "re-organizational," it was the week before classes started when the entire Corps of Cadets returned from summer training and settled into their new rooms and companies. The freshmen, called plebes at West Point, got their full dose of hazing for the first time during Re-Orgy week.

Jan and her classmates were yearlings now, or sophomores to everyone who lived in the real world. They just finished "the best summer of their lives" at Camp Buckner. It *was* the best summer they would have as cadets but certainly not the best summer they might have attending the University of Michigan or Ohio State or Boston College.

That was okay though. They had signed up for this stuff. They could still resign anytime until the first day of classes cow (junior) year and not have any commitment to the military. Jan planned to use every bit of that time before making a definitive decision about staying. If she showed up to the first class next year, however, she would be required to serve five years in the Army after graduation.

That's assuming she survived until then. Since last year, Jan tried not to assume anything anymore.

"Jan, you awake?" Kristi McCarron poked her head in the door.

"I am now, thanks to the bells."

"Great, get dressed so we can grab brunch at the mess hall." Kristi walked into the room and sat in Jan's desk chair.

Jan would have preferred to skip brunch. As upperclassmen, they could always go to Tony's Pizza in the cellar of Building One in Central Area or to Grant Hall for another version of pizza, or burgers. They could even make the longer walk to Ike Hall for still another kind of pizza, burgers or even hotdogs. It seemed that all the meal choices at West Point involved huge portions of Y-chromosome food—pizza, burgers, dogs, chips, nachos, brats and beer. At least the mess hall offered additional choices like steaks, French fries, potatoes, peanut butter, eggs, bacon, sausage, pancakes, creamed chipped beef on toast and bread of every variety by the pound. The only version of salad Jan ever saw involved shredded iceberg lettuce on a large platter soaked in Italian dressing. Fresh fruit was practically nonexistent, although occasionally they could find a banana or an apple, usually offered at breakfast.

"Well, wouldn't want to miss brunch," Jan groaned as she stood up.

All yearlings had been assigned to new companies at the start of the academic year. It was a way of giving them a fresh start after the hardest year of their lives. It certainly helped in Jan and Kristi's case, given that they had been involved in the death of a firstie (senior cadet) last year. Even though First Regiment was considered the harshest of the four, Jan welcomed the move to Company G-1.

Kristi's room was located upstairs in Company H-1. Jan felt grateful that they were not in the same company again. To overcome their past, she felt it was best for them to be separated. This way they could both start over, fresh, with new company mates and hopefully, in time, new friends.

Still, being only one floor apart and having shared a harrowing experience last year, they continued to be an inseparable duo.

"The dicks have struck again," Kristi announced.

Jan walked over to her closet. "What this time?"

Kristi sighed. "Someone peed in my shoes."

"Are you kidding me?" Jan slid a thin gray polyester bathrobe over her t-shirt and underwear. "What's wrong with these people?"

This was Kristi's second incident since the end of Buckner. On the first day back from summer, she discovered a dead snake on her bed when she returned from dinner.

Jan slipped on a pair of flip-flops, grabbed a towel and a bra. "Remember, the superintendent said we should expect these kinds of things."

"I guess I had expected the silent treatment or maybe even a few ugly comments. I didn't expect dead snakes and piss in my shoes."

"It's probably not going to last, Kissy. Just 'keep cool and carry on,' as they say."

"It's 'keep calm and carry on,'" Kristi said.

"Right, whatever." Jan turned to grab the doorknob. "Be right back," she said as she headed to the women's latrine down the hall.

Kristi looked at Jan's roommate's bed. "You want to come with us, Myrna?" she asked the lump under the Gray Girl.

"Nah, I'm going to go back to sleep." Myrna, a cow, or junior cadet, had shared a room with the other two female cows in G-1 all last year. They didn't have to do that again if one of them roomed with a yearling. Myrna must have drawn the short straw. Or she chose it.

Myrna was about five feet two inches tall and all muscle. She kept her hair unusually short, shorter than what the regulation required for women's haircuts. With her man-style hair and her body type, she could easily be mistaken for a male cadet.

Jan retuned from the latrine to find Kristi lying on her bed, feet up, hands interlocked behind her head, resting on Jan's pillow. "Please, Kissy, make yourself at home," Jan said sarcastically.

"Oh, thanks, that's what I did," Kristi said without the slightest reservation.

Sometimes Jan felt irritated when Kristi seemed to assume their friendship was indestructible, almost as if Jan would accept her no matter what she said or did. Jan didn't plan on abandoning her friend, of course, but she wished Kristi would sometimes act like she would. "Okay, let's go, I'm starving."

They entered the mess hall at 1155 hours just as a waiter started to close the massive oak doors.

"Just made it," Jan said.

"A minute later and we would have been screwed over," Kristi said.

They made their way to one of the four hundred tables that filled the three wings of the cavernous, cathedral-style mess hall. Jan still felt awe and admiration every time she entered Washington Hall. As plebes, they weren't allowed to look around and take in its grandeur. Now, as she walked to the last open table set up for brunch, she observed the high cross-beamed ceilings, the fifty state flags, and the magnificent mural covering the entire south wall. The painting depicts the weapons of warfare used in twenty decisive battles. The artist, Mr. T. Loftin Johnson, covered almost 2,500 square feet when he finished his masterpiece in 1936.

This space, more than any other at West Point, gave Jan the feeling that she was truly a member of the Long Gray Line. In the mess hall, Jan felt like she belonged, as if the ghosts of West Point were pleased to see her walk through their hallowed ground. Washington Hall always seemed to welcome her and she gave a silent word of gratitude for its embrace.

Sunday brunch was the only meal with open seating and the two women sat at a table with five plebes, two more yearlings and a cow table commander. The bottom end plebe began filling the plastic cups with ice. The one on the left end shouted, "sir, the dessert for brunch today is chocolate eclairs, would anyone not care for chocolate eclairs, sir?" Plebes usually got a break from having to cut dessert on Sundays, a gift from the wait staff.

The plebe on the right end shouted, "sir, the drink for brunch today is iced tea. Would anyone not care for iced tea, sir?" No one objected, so the fourth-class cadets began filling the plastic cups with the brown liquid and passing them up the table. The table commander was Steve Meyer, Jan's squad leader from first semester last year in H-3. Mary Stenigen, the yearling to his right, had been in their neighboring company G-3. There was a familiar, flirtatious manner between them.

They appear to know each other a little too well.

Jan saw Steve's hand touch Mary's when she handed him the glass of ice tea. Jan and Kristi exchanged pleasantries with Steve and Mary while passing the big plates of food. This time it was pancakes, sausages, hash browns and canned peaches in a bowl. The meal seemed to take a downward turn with the last item and Jan wished the cooks would just put out bananas, oranges or apples instead of the canned stuff. As she thought about making a formal request for fresh fruit, she noticed Mary's hand graze over Steve's while passing the hash browns.

They are a couple! They must have been fraternizing last year. I never noticed.

"Hey Jan, what happened to Angel Trane?" Mary blurted the question.

"What do you mean?" Jan hadn't heard anything about Angel, her roommate all last year in H-3.

"Didn't you hear she quit?"

"What? No, I didn't hear that." Jan stabbed a pancake with her fork, thinking Mary had been misinformed. "Are you sure?"

Come to think of it, Jan had not seen Angel since the summer at Camp Buckner. She assumed that was due to being in different companies and having different schedules.

"Yes, she quit just before the end of Buckner." Mary seemed to enjoy dispensing this information. "She just disappeared one day and never came back."

"Are you kidding? Angel never mentioned wanting to quit and I am pretty sure she would have told me if she did." Jan still didn't believe it.

"It's true. Have you talked to her at all since the summer?" Mary asked.

"No." Jan felt bad about that. "But Angel is always so squared away. She's one of the few cadets who actually loves it here, a real Gray Hog."

"I know! That's why it's so surprising. And no one seems to know why she left. Or no one's telling anyway," Mary replied.

"I just can't believe Angel would quit." Jan wondered why her former roommate had never mentioned wanting to leave. They had been together all plebe year, the most stressful time at West Point, when they relied on each other for everything. Every day from mid-August until the end of May, Jan and Angel prepared their room for inspections, shined shoes, memorized Poop, dressed each other for formations, celebrated milestones, and encouraged each other when the upperclassmen were bearing down on them. They did all of this and more, SO much more, together.

So how could she leave without telling me?

They had come from different worlds. Angel, a petite black girl from Queens, was the first in her family to go to college. When her family visited, they rode a bus to Highland Falls and then walked the mile and a half to the barracks area. Angel sometimes seemed relieved to be at West Point, almost as if it rescued her from being somewhere worse. Jan knew Angel's family had been evicted from their home once.

Or was it twice?

On the other hand, Jan came from a middle-class family in an all-white New Hampshire town. The Wishart family drove one of the two family cars to visit Jan at West Point. And while Angel seemed to enjoy cadet life, Jan hated it.

If I could, I'd go to any other college in a New Orleans minute.

Despite their differences, Jan and Angel had shared an awful lot together—emphasis on *awful*—as plebe year tended to be pretty miserable.

Why didn't she say anything to me? Did Angel think I wouldn't understand?

Jan ate the rest of her brunch in silence watching Steve and Mary flirt and wondering about Angel.

What else did I not notice last year?

THREE

But an officer on duty knows no one—to be partial is to dishonor both himself and the object of his ill-advised favor. (from Worth's Battalion Orders)

August 25, 1982
1150 hours

"SIR, THERE ARE TEN MINUTES UNTIL LUNCH FORMATION. THE MENU FOR LUNCH IS: CHICKEN HOAGIES, POTATO CHIPS, CARROT STICKS AND LEMONADE. THE UNIFORM FOR BREAKFAST IS CLASS UNIFORM! TEN MINUTES, SIR!"

The plebe minute caller stood shouting under the clock in the hallway as Jan returned to her room following morning classes. After calling the ten-minute bell, the plebe returned to his room to wait five minutes. All other fourth classmen were already outside at formation where the upperclassmen inspected and tested them on their plebe "poop" or required knowledge. Jan wasn't in a hurry to haze the plebes. There were plenty of others who could do that.

As she placed her books in height order on the bookshelf above her desk, she thought about how she could contact Angel.

I never even got her address. No phone number either.

Jan felt bad for not acquiring this information, yet cadets didn't usually exchange home addresses and phone numbers—why would they ever need that?

Jan smiled as she recalled when Angel invited her to a "Cultural Affairs Seminar (CAS)" meeting last year. "It's about hair and skin care," Angel had said. Jan had nothing better to do that night and she figured she could use a few beauty tips.

They left their room, pinged along the walls and squared every corner until they exited the building and crossed Central Area. They continued to ping until they reached the staircase leading into a vertical rock wall behind the mess hall. After climbing a hundred or so steps, they arrived at the Cadet Chapel. Then they descended a flight of stairs to the basement room where the CAS members were gathering.

As soon as Jan rounded the corner into the room, she realized she should have asked a few more questions about CAS. Apparently, it was a club for black cadets.

How did I miss that?

The room was filled with various shades of brown complexions. Jan's was the only pale face, and she felt it tingle, turning bright red while she looked very intently at the snack table in the back of the room. She actually thought that if she didn't look at anyone, maybe they wouldn't notice her, either.

Yet Leslie Wright, Jan's Cadet Basic Training roommate, was also in attendance. Leslie shouted from across the room, "Wishart, the powdered donuts are for you."

Everyone erupted in laughter making Jan feel much better.

The plebe returned to the hallway clock to call the five-minute bell as Jan walked out her door toward Leslie's room.

The three other yearling women in G-1—Leslie Wright, Lisa Techtton and Esther Gonsalez—shared a two-person room. Jan entered without knocking, "Leslie, did you know Angel quit after Buckner?"

"Good thing I wasn't naked, Wishart," Leslie said while sitting on her bed, bent over and tying her shoelaces. Esther and Lisa had already left for formation.

"You wouldn't be naked this close to formation," Jan argued. "Did you know about Angel?"

"The point is, you are supposed to knock first, Wishart." Leslie didn't look up from her task.

"Okay, Leslie, sorry I didn't knock. Now can you tell me about Angel, please?"

"I don't know anything about it," Leslie said.

"Why would she quit? Angel was practically Miss West Point. Her family was so proud of her, she never got any demerits, she got decent grades, she was doing fine." Jan could not think of one reason why Angel would just up and quit. "Have you heard anything about what happened?"

"Why would I hear anything? You know her better than I do."

"I just thought you might know more since you were in CAS together. And weren't you both in the gospel choir?" Jan asked.

"Wishart, every black cadet joins the gospel choir. It's mandatory," Leslie said as if it was common knowledge.

"Why's it mandatory?"

"It's a support system, it's how we help each other."

"Oh." She tried to think of a similar support system that she could join. Nothing came to mind.

"I mean, there's only so many of us, you know?"

"Yeah, I guess so. Angel never said anything about that. Would anyone in your support system have her address or phone number?"

"Yeah, someone might. I'll see what I can find out."

"Thanks, Leslie." Jan turned toward the door. She and Leslie had been roommates all through Cadet Basic Training, better known as "Beast." They had survived seven weeks of hell together. Yet Jan hadn't managed to bond with her like she had with Angel.

She turned to face Leslie again. "And don't you think we can start calling each other by our first names now that we're yearlings?"

Leslie stood up and placed her hat on her head. "Go for it, Wishart."

The plebes had started calling the two-minute bell when Jan and Leslie walked outside to lunch formation. She found her place in Third Squad, Second Platoon and waited for the platoon sergeant, Cadet John Heggenbach, to call them to attention. Instead, he walked toward Jan.

"Cadet Wishart, as an assistant squad leader I expect you to be out here at the ten-minute bell to supervise your plebes."

Dammit. "Yes, sorry about that," Jan replied. He had a way of making her feel nervous, like Cadet Jackson did last year.

"I don't want you to be sorry about it, I want you to do something about it," he said scornfully. "If you cannot do your job, we can get someone else who will."

Oh God, not another stick-up-your-ass type. Jan decided not to push his buttons. "I understand. It won't happen again." That seemed to satisfy him as he walked back to the front of the formation. *Where he belongs!*

After lunch and a quick trip to her room to brush her teeth, Jan made her way to her first afternoon class, physics. She dreaded it more than all other math, science and history classes. Languages were her only strength. She earned A's in English last year, which was practically unheard of for many plebes. She also did extremely well in Arabic. Jan wondered how she managed to get an A learning a language with funny looking letters that reads right to left, while barely maintaining a C in American History.

She walked into the physics class and chose the desk smack in the center of the room.

Not too close and not too far from the professor's desk.

Jan believed the middle was the best place to hide. It was impossible for female cadets to blend in completely, but by staying away from the edges, sides, ends and corners, she felt less likely to stand out.

I always wanted to stand out in high school and at home. Not here.

The room soon filled with her classmates. One was Rick Davidson. Last year, he had been a company mate in H-3. She had considered him to be a stuck-up, self-centered, prior-service Mr. Know-It-All until she discovered that he was also a sensitive, concerned, and deeply religious friend. Furthermore, he tried to save her from harassment by two firsties last May. It all backfired, however, and she was charged with two Honor violations because of Rick Davidson's actions. She had to defend herself at a cadet-run Honor Board. All that was bad enough, although it wasn't the worst part.

What a disaster that was.

Jan didn't like to remember that time. It was one of those things she wanted to stay in the past. She lived through it, she learned a lot, and she didn't ever want to think about it again. That's how Jan felt about all of plebe year, especially the last month of plebe year.

Rick sat down at the desk next to hers. She nodded at him and he smiled at her. They had spoken a couple of times at Buckner and only briefly in this class. They couldn't seem to find the easy rhythm they had last year—when she didn't fully know him. Jan wasn't sure why they kept misfiring. She wanted to talk with him again like she did in their letters. She just couldn't seem to get that level of comfort with him in person.

"How are you faring so far?" he asked, knowing physics was not her strong suit.

"Okay, but I'm sure I'll need help again," she said, remembering how he helped her pass calculus last year. *And Survival Swimming*.

Rick Davidson was good at everything and that was part of the problem for Jan. He was extremely handsome, athletic, smart, funny and seemingly popular among their classmates. His prior service record and combat patch gave him an almost god-like status among the Corps. Very few cadets had combat patches.

"Fine, I'll help you in this class and you can help me with papers." He smiled at her.

"I can't *write* your papers for you," she said. Most cadets pulled all-nighters when a paper was due. Jan knocked out her papers in a couple of hours. Her roommates were always jealous when she climbed into her rack while they continued to labor away.

"No, I wouldn't expect you to do that. But you could proofread for grammar and spelling and help with the overall flow, right?"

"Well...yes, I can help with that." She didn't want to commit too much. It was good to have one thing that she could do better than most.

Better than him, especially.

"Class attention!" The cadets popped out of their seats and stood at attention while their physics professor entered the room. The "P" walked to his desk dropping books, binders and notepads.

"Be seated," he commanded. He walked to the chalkboard and wrote, "Section Test Next Friday." Then he pulled out the class roster and called their names out loud.

"Present, sir," Jan responded when her name was called. With everyone accounted for, Major Stanley instructed the class to take boards. Cadets stood and moved to the chalkboard that enveloped the interior walls of the room. Jan stood next to Rick, picked up a piece of chalk and prepared to write an equation.

"A person is stuck inside a falling elevator, whose cable broke ten meters above the ground. Let's say the person wants to cancel out their final velocity by jumping exactly when the elevator hits the bottom." Major Stanley walked the inner perimeter of cadets as he spoke.

I've always wondered if this was possible.

The professor continued, "Write the equations to answer these three questions: How long after the cable breaks would the person need to jump? At what velocity (relative to the elevator) would the person need to jump? And, if the person were to jump at this velocity on stable ground, how high would they go? Is this even reasonable?"

That's four questions.

Jan began to write on her chalkboard, but quickly stopped. She had no idea how to proceed. She noticed Rick had stopped writing on his board also.

Wow, is he actually struggling with something?

Major Stanley gave additional hints, which allowed Jan to make some headway on her equation. She figured out that the elevator would hit the bottom in 1.43 seconds. She struggled with the second equation while Rick had already moved onto the third question.

Major Stanley stood between the two of them. "Nice work, Mr. Davidson." Facing the board, Jan continued to work on her second equation until she felt the professor standing close behind her.

Too close.

She felt his breath on her neck. Her right hand holding the chalk froze on the board at head level. She felt her body go rigid as he pressed his body even closer to hers.

He placed his left hand on her left hip, holding her in place. "Miss Wishart, you already have the time until impact. All you need now," he placed his right hand over her right at the chalkboard, "is to times that by gravity." Moving her hand with the chalk, he wrote the equation on her board while pressing his groin into her butt. She could feel his erection as he rubbed himself against her buttocks.

Fuck!

She couldn't move. She stood there, like a statue, waiting for him to back away. He didn't seem to be in any hurry.

Freak!

Yet Jan still couldn't move. She couldn't even think. It was as if his rubbing had immobilized her brain.

Major Stanley moved her hand, writing the second equation and when he started the third, he whispered in her right ear, "I'd be happy to tutor you sometime after class." He let go of her hand, which promptly fell to her side. She felt him turn around and walk to the other side of the room. "Everyone back to your desks," he said after a short delay.

Jan placed the chalk in the tray then walked to her chair. Everything else seemed perfectly normal. Major Stanley wrote the homework assignment on the board while everyone took out pencils to copy it down. Jan began to wonder what just happened—did her professor really just rub himself against her and proposition her?

Or did I just imagine that?

It seemed like hours before class ended. Jan hurriedly gathered her things and rushed out of the classroom. Halfway down the hallway, she heard Rick Davidson running toward her. "Jan, you forgot your hat."

She turned to face him as he caught up to her. He held out her gray class hat, the one Jan called an "envelope."

"Thanks." She snatched it out of his hand and turned back the way she was going.

"Hey, what's wrong?"

"Nothing." She started "pinging," or walking extremely fast, just like the plebes.

"Why so grouchy, then?" He tried to keep up with her. "And what's your damn hurry? You got a plane to catch or something?"

She stopped suddenly. "Didn't you see what happened in there?"

"In where?"

"For Christ's sake, Rick! In physics class."

"Jan, everyone struggled with..."

"Not that, Rick," she shouted at him.

Rick furrowed his brows in confusion while Jan glared at him.

How could he not have noticed? "You *had* to have seen *that.*"

"Seen what?"

"Really?" she asked almost jokingly. "You really didn't see what Major Stanley just did in class?"

Rick shook his head slightly and tried to recall the professor's actions, "he wrote on the board, he gave us homework, he..."

"What he did to me, Rick, to me!" His obliviousness made her even angrier.

Rick shrugged his shoulders. "Obviously, I missed something..."

"While we were at boards?" Jan said, trying to help Rick's recollection. "He stood behind me, remember?" She seemed to be pleading with him. "I was right next to you, Rick. Right. Goddamn. Next. To. You!"

Rick continued to look dumbfounded. "Sorry, Jan, but I have no idea what I was supposed to have noticed. I'm not a mind reader, you know."

"Ugh!" She rolled her eyes, turned away from him and continued pinging down the hallway.

FOUR

I will never accept defeat.
I will never quit.
I will never leave a fallen comrade.
(from A Soldier's Creed)

August 25, 1982
1530 hours

Maybe Angel just had enough of this shit, Jan thought as she scurried back to her room. In some ways, she envied everyone who quit. They could go to a normal college and live a normal life.

After plopping her books down on her desk, she changed into her athletic uniform: black shorts, white Academy crested t-shirt, with white tube socks and court sneakers. She continued to think about Angel even as she headed to Team Handball practice.

Team Handball was one of those obscure sports that attracted basketball, soccer and baseball jocks who were not good enough to make the Corps Squad (Varsity) teams. A cousin to basketball, Team Handball is played on an indoor court by passing and shooting a slightly smaller than normal volleyball. Each team fields five players and a goalie to protect the net. The players pass the ball down the court until it's within range to shoot at the goal.

This turned out to be a good fit for Jan who spent her high school years playing basketball. She knew how to pass and shoot. And since no one actually played Team Handball before arriving at West Point, she didn't need expertise, only potential.

"We are going to have a great team this year," Captain Hasuko announced before practice. Since it takes almost a year to learn how to play the sport, once you made the Team Handball Team, you could stay on it for your entire cadet career. "We've got a couple plebes who look to be ringers. And we did so well last year that I expect we will do even better this year." Both men's and women's Team Handball teams made it to Nationals last year. Of course, it had something to do with the fact that very few other colleges had even heard of Team Handball. The Europeans were their only real competition.

Jan leaned over to her teammate, Pepper, and whispered, "Are we going to DC again this year?" Jan had a blast on the DC trip last year and she welcomed any excuse to leave West Point for a while.

"Looks like it," Pepper said. Jan didn't know Pepper's real name; no one seemed to know it.

They started running drills up and down one end of the court. Jan glanced at the other end where the men's team started practicing. Rick Davidson had joined the Team Handball team at the end of last year. Jan saw him passing and shooting the ball with what seemed like ease and coordination. He also had to learn the sport from scratch. Yet he played like someone who grew up playing, even lettering in Team Handball.

Of course, everything comes easy for him.

In between passing and shooting drills, Jan tried to figure out her feelings for Rick. Truthfully, she practically loved him. Not only did he help her pass calculus and Survival Swimming, he also saved her ass in a big way. She had totally misjudged him, along with a few other people.

Her problem with Rick Davidson was that she didn't know how to get close to him. Furthermore, Jan never understood the art of flirting. *Nothing cute comes in five foot ten.* She felt awkward when she tried to be "cute," or whatever it was that made for flirtatious behavior. She figured she would need a whole lot of luck landing a boyfriend—Rick or anyone else.

Yet as she watched him running the Team Handball drills, she regretted their last encounter after physics class. She didn't mean to be rude. If she only had a few hours to calm down, she could have gently told Rick what happened.

I blew it again. She resolved to walk back to the barracks with Rick after Team Handball practice and try again. *This time, I'll say something "cute."*

Instead, she asked him if he knew why Angel quit.

"I thought maybe you knew, Jan," he said.

"She never said anything to me about quitting, but then again, I didn't see much of her last summer."

"No, I mean, I *thought you knew."*

Jan didn't get what he was hinting at. "Knew *what,* Rick?" She could feel her patience dwindling again.

"Well, I can't say for sure. I only know what the rumor mill says."

Jan wondered who was in the "rumor mill"; apparently not her. "What have you heard?"

Rick stopped walking and faced Jan. "Rumor has it that she's pregnant."

Jan gaped at Rick. *What?* "Run that by me again, please."

He shrugged his shoulders. "That's what I heard anyway."

"No. Angel is definitely not pregnant," Jan said. *Unless I've totally misjudged her, too.* "She is the most religious person I know. She never had or even mentioned a boyfriend. And she's even more..." Jan stopped short, realizing that she did not want to share certain information with Rick just yet. "She's even more…picky…than I am when it comes to guys."

"Yeah, well, Jan, I hate to break it to you. But even good girls get pregnant."

Jan hated that kind of statement. *As if women got pregnant all by themselves.* She decided right then, right there, that she would get birth control so that when, *IF*, she ever had sex, she would be protected. At least from becoming pregnant, which in her mind was the worst thing that could happen from having sex. "Yes, Rick, she could be pregnant. I'm just saying, it's not likely to have happened to the Angel I knew." *Then again, what the hell do I know about anyone anymore.*

FIVE

SLUG, n. A special punishment for a serious offense.
(A Glossary of Cadet Slang, Bugle Notes, 1981, p.293)

August 28, 1982
1545 hours

Jan wrapped the starched white belts over her dress gray and across her chest. She hooked the crisscrossed belts in place using the small brass breastplate, shined to perfection. She slid another white belt around her waist, securing the bayonet on her right hip and the cartridge box just above her buttocks. She placed her gray saucer cap on her head and looked in the mirror.

Kristi came barging in the door wearing the exact same uniform. Only she was about a foot shorter than Jan and more compact. Together, they looked a little like Lucy and Ethel in costume.

"You ready to take a walk on the wild side?" Kristi asked.

After classes on Friday, most cadets prepared for the weekend activities. Some upperclassmen could leave Post until late Sunday afternoon—something akin to being let out of prison for two days. Others prepared to go on team trips or to dinner with their sponsors' families. Sponsors, Army officers assigned to every cadet, were supposed to invite them to dinner or family events whenever possible. Jan's sponsor had never initiated contact with her. Still other cadets prepared to go to Ike or Grant Hall for a few beers and limited socialization with other cadets. Plebes had the exciting option of Cullum Hall, if it was open.

Jan and Kristi had to walk the area. Each had been slapped with one hundred hour slugs or walking tours at the end of last year. This was their punishment for being out after Taps in an unauthorized area. Jan figured it was a small price to pay, considering what had happened.

They had managed to walk about twenty-five hours before the end of last year. They were allowed to walk another thirty hours at Buckner and they had walked about twenty more since returning to Woo Poo U. Now they were winding down the last twenty-five hours, which seemed like nothing compared to where they started. It reminded Jan of that old saying: *The journey of a thousand miles begins with the first step.* She felt like she had already walked those thousand miles, step by step by step by step.

They made their way to Central Area where all the Area Birds were forming up for inspection. Both Jan and Kristi made sure they had everything right: highly shined leather shoes and brass breastplate; M-14 rifle completely cleaned; and haircut above the bottom edge of the dress gray collar. If they didn't pass inspection there was a good chance they could get even more demerits or area tours.

They did pass inspection, however, and they began pacing on the hard pavement until they reached one gray barracks wall. Then they executed an about face, turning 180 degrees before marching to the other gray barracks wall. They would repeat this mindless ritual for two hours until they were dismissed. Then they would go back to their rooms, pull off the belts, put away their rifles and go back outside for dinner formation. After dinner they would stay on room confinement for the rest of the night, only being allowed to go to the latrine or the library. They would do the whole process all over again on Saturday after classes, parade, room inspection and whatever else was required.

Jan had made her fourth about face when another cadet walking the area, only a few paces to her right, whispered loudly, "Murderer!"

She froze momentarily, then quickly regained her composure by moving the rifle from her right to her left shoulder. She slowed her pace so that the insulting cadet could get slightly ahead of her. She wanted to see his face the next time he turned around. She wanted him to see her face, too.

She kept slowing down until he was about five feet ahead and slightly right of her. He stopped at the barracks wall but didn't execute an about face. He stayed facing the gray granite stones. If she reached the wall before he turned around, she would not be able to see his face. It seemed that was his plan.

Jan reached the barracks wall without getting a look at him. "Coward!" She made sure she said it plenty loud enough.

They turned around at the same time. He probably planned to stay parallel to her so she couldn't identify him. She would keep trying to get a look at him before their little walk ended.

A short way down Central Area, Kristi also marched back and forth from one gray stone building to the other. Another cadet slightly behind and to her left whispered, "Hey, are you Kristi McCarron?

"Maybe. Who wants to know?" Kristi replied without moving her head.

Talking while on walking tours was not allowed. Yet with enough practice, cadets became proficient in carrying on full-length conversations while appearing to be stone silent. Plebes were often caught because they hadn't learned the art of talking without moving their mouths. By yearling year and with enough area tours, most cadets mastered it.

They kept walking at the same pace, only a couple of steps apart. "You're kind of famous."

"Good famous? Or bad famous?"

"Probably not good. But maybe not as bad as you might think."

"Why's that?" Kristi slowed her pace until he was even with her.

"Well, there are a lot of women on Post who feel safe again."

"And why's that?"

"There were a few other victims, you know, before the one you guys found." The anonymous cadet seemed to have inside information.

"How many?"

"Don't know for sure, but at least three, I've heard."

"How do you know?"

"Let's just say I have connections."

"Why is everything so secretive?" Kristi asked, "Why haven't we been told the full story?"

"The full story will never be told. You'll just have to be satisfied with knowing not everyone is against you. Or the other gal."

"Jan?"

"Yeah, her. A lot of people are very grateful to you both. But no one is going to tell you that."

"What's your name?"

"Sorry, that's classified."

"Fall out!" The cadet in charge of the area shouted the command signaling they were free to go to their rooms. Jan and Kristi sauntered toward the New South ramp. They told each other about their respective conversations before reaching the barracks and ascending the upperclassmen's stairwell. Plebes were required to use the far stairwell at the other end of the building. Jan wasn't a fan of the rule because she had been chastised for using the wrong stairwell last year in Old South.

Oh well, that's the way the brownie crumbles.

Kristi kept going up the stairs to the third floor, while Jan peeled off at the second floor heading to her corner room, located at the end of a short hallway that branched off the end of the main hallway. She opened the door to see Myna embracing another female cadet. They broke apart quickly, almost too quickly. Jan nodded and mumbled "hey" as she placed her M-14 in its wooden rack just inside the door. She concentrated intensely on removing her gloves, not looking at either woman. She felt like she had walked in on something private, something intimate. Yet it was her room, too, and she wasn't required to knock on her own room door.

Jan focused on taking off the white belts. The other female cadet made a quick exit. Jan recognized her as Myrna's classmate from First Battalion and a member of the women's softball team. Jan continued to dismantle her ensemble without looking at Myrna, who sat down at her desk and began leafing through a textbook.

"Jan, Sandy was upset about some news she received from her family. I was just trying to comfort her."

"Okay," Jan replied, wondering why Myrna felt the need to explain.

Jan hugged Kristi and Angel only once last year after they successfully finished the Indoor Obstacle Course Test (IOCT). With everything they had been through during plebe year, and even in the aftermath of "the event," they never hugged each other. Now that Jan thought about it, they probably should have comforted each other more often. It just wasn't something they ever did.

None of my business. If Myrna wanted to hug another woman, fine. Jan would not question it. She would not tell anyone what she saw. She would not give it another thought. Even though she knew damn well Myrna was a lesbian and technically not even supposed to even be in the Army, Jan would not do anything about it. She wasn't a snitch.

SIX

Deep into that darkness peering,
long I stood there wondering, fearing,
Doubting,
dreaming dreams no mortals ever dared to dream before
(From The Raven, by Edgar Allan Poe, West Point cadet in 1830)

September 12, 1982
0845 hours

She is climbing a small hill. The sun is shining, the grass is green and the trees are swaying in the breeze. She is alone but she doesn't mind. Everything feels fine. She is light, strong and carefree.

A shape comes into her peripheral vision. She turns her head and sees a man in a gray suit climbing the hill, about fifty yards away. She doesn't know the man.

It's okay, he can climb the hill too, she says to herself.

Another man in gray comes into view on her left, about thirty yards away. She doesn't know him either. Still, she doesn't mind.

Soon more and more men begin to show up, all wearing the same gray suit. She looks at her own clothes. She is wearing all red.

It's getting a little crowded on this hill, she thinks.

All the other climbers are men, not one other woman nor any children. She doesn't feel quite as good as she did when she was alone. The men continue to grow in number. First a few, then dozens and now hundreds of gray men are climbing the hill. They close in around her. They are right beside her, on her left, her right, in front and behind. She wonders where they came from and how they grew so quickly in number.

They are climbing the hill in step now—left, right, left—like soldiers marching in a parade. She doesn't want to keep in step with the men. She wants to be on the hill by herself again, climbing at her own pace. But she cannot slow down, she cannot turn around and she cannot run away. They have hemmed her in. She cannot escape.

She sees one man pull out a bow and arrow. Then another does the same, then another, and another, and another. Each one pulls out a bow and arrow. Soon every man has a bow and arrow.

But she has a weapon, too. She has a knife—a big hunting knife.

She knows the gray men want to hit the bulls-eye with their arrows. They all want to strike the red spot in the center of the massive columns of gray. She knows they will aim for her.

So she attacks first. She stabs the man on her left, then she stabs the one on her right, then she stabs the one in front of her. She turns around and stabs the one behind her. She stabs and stabs and stabs until they are all dead.

As she looks across the hill of dead men, bells begin ringing...

Jan twitched awake. The Cadet Chapel bells rang out from their perch above West Point, breaking into another one of her nightmares. She still hated when they woke her up every Sunday morning, yet she couldn't complain when they cut off a bad dream. She noticed this happening more and more often, which left her in the peculiar position of feeling slightly grateful for the bells.

She got dressed, ran upstairs and barged into her old roommate's room. "Kristi, after brunch, I'm going to stop by H-3. Wanna come with me?"

Kristi's new roommates were still in bed. Pamela Pearson, from Texas, had the physique of a racehorse: wide shoulders, tanned, muscled arms, sinewy legs with what looked like small boulders under the skin behind her calves. Her pretty face was the capstone on a bronzed sculpture. Jan thought she must have a lot of admirers.

The other roommate, Violet Carpetta, was the total opposite. At Camp Buckner, Violet had a solid build; she had the body type of most female cadets—thick, strong and muscular. Recently, however, Jan noticed she had lost a lot of weight. Violet looked almost too thin now. Her once strong arms were beginning to look like toothpicks. Her legs had lost their chiseled tone. Her form-fitted uniform now draped off her body like a bathrobe. Jan wondered if Violet might be sick, really sick, like cancer-kind-of-sick.

The week prior, Jan had questioned Violet on her appearance. "Are you okay, Violet? Do you need to go on sick call?"

"I'm fine," she answered tersely.

"It's just that you're looking really thin. You're losing a lot of weight."

"That doesn't mean I'm sick, Jan."

"No, I know, but it looks like..."

"You're just jealous because you can't lose weight."

Jan had been verbally punched in the face. She decided she would not question Violet again. Besides, being too thin was always better than being too heavy for women at West

Point. It was true that Jan wished she could be thinner. Almost every female cadet wanted to be smaller and those who actually were thin probably still felt too fat.

"I can think of a million other things I would rather do than visit our plebe company," Kristi stated. "Are you out of your ever-loving mind?"

Jan knew it would be harder for Kristi to visit H-3 than anyone else. "I don't plan to stay long, I just need to see if anyone knows about Angel."

"Maybe she just wanted to leave, Jan. She's not the only one who quit since last year," Pamela protested.

"Angel is not the quitting type. She did well plebe year, she was squared away and she wanted to graduate. She was proud to be a cadet. I'm convinced she didn't leave by choice...something had to have happened." Jan had given it a lot of thought by then.

"Well, maybe something did happen, maybe something private. She might have gotten pregnant for instance. She wouldn't exactly broadcast that news," Kristi said.

"Did you hear the same rumor as Rick? I can't believe you would even think that, Kissy. You know Angel didn't get pregnant. She was even more virginal than me." *Angel probably never even kissed a guy.*

"Okay, well, I don't think it would be wise for me to go to H-3 today."

"Understand. Pamela, what about you? Are you willing to go with me to H-3 after brunch?" Jan asked.

"Sure, but only if you show me your old room. I want to see where the legend began," Pamela replied with a smirk.

Pamela seemed fascinated with Jan and Kristi's past, often asking them to recount the events from last May. She was one of those rare cadets who felt proud to be their friend, rather than being repulsed or fearful of them.

"Better get a move on, then. I'm starving and you know they won't hold the doors open one minute past noon," Jan said.

Once Kristi and Pamela were ready, the three women walked to the mess hall for Sunday brunch. Violet declined to go, stating she was too tired to get out of bed.

Then maybe you should eat something.

After brunch, Pamela and Jan climbed the steps of Central Barracks to the third floor, Company H-3. Since it was early afternoon, many cadets were still asleep or had gone back to sleep after brunch. For this reason, the barracks were always oddly quiet on Sundays.

Jan felt the familiar anxiety of plebe year creep into her spine, down her legs, until even her toes seemed to tingle from fear. The only good thing about last year was "Amen-oh-yay-ah," Jan's term for the cessation of the menstrual cycle due to stress. She also broke out with skin rashes. Some women suffered hair loss.

How did we ever live through it?

Jan remembered hearing about people who had survived catastrophic events only to have nervous breakdowns later from the memories. She kind of understood the feeling as she walked through the halls of H-3. She found Cadet Rallins' door and knocked softly. The other nametag read "Petersen," the only other firstie woman in H-3.

"Come in," said a groggy voice.

"Hey, Jean," Jan said trying to act like it was perfectly normal to call her by her first name, "I need to talk to you. Do you have a minute?"

Cadet Rallins had obviously just woken up and was still in a t-shirt and underwear. She was a beautiful woman with a gorgeous shape. Jan often wondered how she had survived this long at West Point and what may or may not have happened to her along the way. A lump in the other bed indicated Linda Petersen was still sleeping.

"Uh, okay. Lemme just throw on my sweats."

"Sure. This is my friend from H-1, Pamela Pearson." Jan motioned toward her classmate. They greeted each other with a nod. Jan got right to the point. "Well, I just wanted to see if you knew about Angel Trane."

"Knew what?" Jean asked.

Jean Rallins had been Angel's second semester squad leader last year. "Obviously you don't know she quit over the summer. I didn't know either until re-orgy week. I'm trying to contact her, but no one seems to know her address or phone number and I was hoping you might have some information about her. Did you keep a file on her or anything?"

"No, the TAC officers do, though. We have a new TAC this year but Angel's file should still be in the office."

"What happened to Captain Spanner?" Jan asked, remembering how helpful he had been to her and Kristi after the mess they got into last year.

"He was sent to a desk job in the Association of Graduates. Apparently he took the fall for everything that happened." It seemed Jean didn't want to actually say what happened. "We were sorry to see him go. Our new TAC, Captain Morris, is very different."

"How so?" Jan asked, hoping she meant *different in a good way.*

"Well," Cadet Rallins continued, "for instance, he told me I could be company commander next semester and the first woman to have that distinction. I only needed to meet him a few times in his office, if you know what I mean."

Jan knew Jean Rallins could not have escaped this kind of thing. Not with her looks. Not with her body. "Oh, geez. You, too?" Jan asked.

"What? Did this happen to you, Jan?"

"In physics class, while we were at boards, my professor rubbed me the wrong way, literally. He whispered in my ear that he would be happy to tutor me in his office after classes." Jan felt disgusted just saying it. "What do you do in that kind of situation? What did you say to your TAC, Jean?"

Jean walked to her sink cabinet and pulled out her toothbrush. "You have to be absolutely firm. Show no fear. I told Captain Morris that I would rather be the company BP." Barracks Police (BPs) were civilian contractors who cleaned the common areas of the barracks—the latrines, hallways, stairwells, the CQ and day rooms. "It's good if you can shame them while you're at it. Say something about his wife if he's married. I told Captain Morris that he had a very pretty wife and he must be very proud of her." Jean continued, "Of course I've never seen his wife, but that didn't matter. The point is, make him aware that you know he's married—that usually takes care of things right there. If they think you will report them, formally or informally, they're more likely to leave you alone."

"Jean," Pamela spoke this time, "why don't you just *go ahead and report him*, formally?"

That was a good question, Jan thought. *Why don't more women file complaints when this shit happens?*

"Have you ever tried that, Pam?" Jean asked as she squeezed toothpaste onto her toothbrush.

"Well, no. No one has ever bothered me...in that way."

"Well, guess what happens when you report something like this up the chain of command? NO-THING! And in my case, the TAC IS the chain of command. Believe me, I've tried it that way before. At best, the jerk gets a warning. At worst, you get a mark on your back."

Jan figured Jean knew about these things. *She's been around the park a time or two.* Jean was the first female cadet to walk one hundred hours of area tours. Controversy followed her all the way to firstie year. Jan now realized that it probably wasn't all her fault.

"Okay, but my physics P accosted me right in the middle of class with about ten guys in the room. No one seemed to notice. How do I deal with that?" Jan asked.

Jean put her toothbrush down before explaining. "Well, first of all, get at least one of the guys in the class to be an ally. Second, don't ever turn your back on the P. When you take boards, stand at an angle to the board. Be aware of his location at all times. When he approaches you, make some kind of loud noise or other signal to your classmate to watch or intervene. There are guys who will help you out with this if you ask."

Jan never thought about asking for help from male cadets. She always figured she had to handle everything herself. Jean Rallins had just told Jan one secret to success at West Point: *Form alliances with the good guys to keep away the bad guys.*

Jan thanked Jean for her advice, acknowledging she would have to find Angel's information some other way since visiting Captain Morris was now out of the question.

She then led Pamela to her old room. The nametags on the door indicated it was inhabited by plebes again. *It's probably a room no one else wants.* Jan used her knuckles to knock two times on the door— not softly, but not pounding either.

"Enter, sir!"

Jan opened the door to see three male plebes at attention—one black, one Latino and one white. It reminded her that West Point and the Army had come much further on race relations than the rest of America. The Army wasn't a place for segregation—everyone is thrown into the same boat and you must learn to row together.

"Hey, guys. Sorry to bother you on Sunday, but I wanted to show my friend our old plebe room. Do you mind?" Jan knew they could not possibly "mind," she was simply being nice.

"No, ma'am," the black cadet said.

Jan and Pamela entered the room. "See, Pam, just like any other room. Nothing special."

"Oh no, not at all. This room has a vibe. It has an aura," Pamela said while waking toward the windows at the back of the room.

Jan looked at the Latino cadet and raised her eyebrows. He smiled back. "Pamela, let's leave these gentlemen to their homework. This room is as plain and boring as all the rest."

Pamela stood at the windows and closed her eyes. She took in a deep breath. "Can't you feel it?"

"Feel what, Pam?"

The three men remained at attention, their eyes flitting back and forth from Pamela to Jan.

Pamela raised her arms. "Them!"

Jan smirked at the white male this time. "Yes, these guys do have a certain, uh, vibe, about them...a certain olfactory aura...."

Pamela opened her eyes, "No, not them." She closed her eyes again while raising her hands, palms open to the ceiling. "THEM!"

"Okay, Pam, I'm not sure who you mean, but let's go and let these nice young men get back to...."

"Grant, Pershing, MacArthur, Patton, Eisenhower—they all lived in this room, they still visit this room," Pamela whispered.

"Um, I don't think that's statistically possible..." Jan said while winking at the black plebe.

"This room makes the great ones," Pamela continued to whisper. Then she opened her eyes and looked straight at the Latino cadet. "You are going to be very famous one day." She moved her gaze to the black cadet. "And you are going to be the most successful general of your time." She glanced to the white guy. "And your name will be known all over the country someday."

The three male plebes didn't move a muscle, still standing in silence.

"Oh, Pamela, stop with all this nonsense. No one believes in your gift for fortune telling. Now, let's go."

"Okay, fine." Pamela shrugged her shoulders and walked straight out the door to the hallway.

Jan followed, turning to the three plebes before leaving. "Guys, she's full of shit, don't believe a word she says."

"Yes, ma'am," three pairs of wide eyes replied.

Jan and Pamela giggled as they walked down the H-3 hallway. Just before they reached the main stairwell, Chris Barrington exited the men's latrine almost bumping into Jan. Chris was one of the few cadets who refused to speak to Jan and Kristi at Recognition Day last year. He was the kind of cadet the superintendent had warned them about.

"Why the hell are you here, Wishart?" he questioned her as if she was still a plebe.

She almost locked up in the "smack" position out of muscle memory and said, "No excuse sir." Instead, she hesitated long enough to remember she was no longer a *beanhead.* No matter what Barrington thought, she wasn't going let him scare her off. "Hey, Chris, nice to see you again, too," she said calmly even though her stomach began knotting.

"Nothing nice about seeing you, Wishart. Why don't you stay over in First Regiment where you belong?" he seethed.

Jan took her time answering. *I have to appear cool, calm and connected.* "I came to find out why Angel Trane quit. Do you have ideas, *Chris*?" She emphasized his first name.

"Why the hell would I even care, Wishart? You must be mistaking me for someone who gives a damn."

Obviously he still held Jan responsible for everything that went down last year. She was not going to change his mind.

She had been confronted with stares, glares and the occasional disparaging remark, but this was the first time someone openly opposed her. She thought carefully about what to say next.

"Chris, no one is more sorry than me for what happened last year. We certainly didn't plan to hurt anyone. That's the plain and simple truth."

Chris Barrington seemed to think about his response before saying, "The problem with that explanation, Wishart, is that the only person who could tell us another side of the story isn't here anymore."

"If you want to hear more versions of the story, Chris, maybe you should ask some of the women around Post who were raped."

Chris Barrington had heard enough. He wasn't about to let Jan, or anyone else, tarnish his friend's good name. He took a step closer to Jan as if she was a plebe again. "Get the fuck out of here, Wishart. Don't ever step foot in Company H-3 again, you hear me?"

Jan waited a moment. She knew his anger was close to the boiling point, and she didn't want to be standing near him when it blew. Yet she could not let him have the last word. "I was just leaving, Chris. But you don't own the property rights to H-3 or anywhere else on Post. I will go wherever I want."

She and Pamela resumed their walk toward the stairwell. Just before exiting the hallway, Chris Barrington shouted, "Fair warning, Wishart, don't venture this way again."

SEVEN

All oppression creates a state of war.
(Simone de Beauvoir)

September 13, 1982
1300 hours

Jan walked with Rick to physics class so she could calmly tell him what Major Stanley had done and ask for his help should it occur again. She decided to take Jean Rallins' advice and solicit help from one of the best guys she knew in order to keep the creep, Major Stanley, at least one arm's distance away from her. When she told him what their physics professor had previously done, Rick became incensed.

"Who the fuck does he think he is?" Rick shouted.

"Shhh, Rick, calm down."

"No, I won't calm down. I'm going to tell that bastard to keep his hands to himself."

"Well," Jan said, "it wasn't exactly his hands that were the problem."

"Jan, this isn't funny." He was right about that.

"I know, Rick, but we have to find humor in these things or we'd all go crazy. Besides," she continued, "we're going to put a stop to it, right?"

"We most certainly are," Rick affirmed. "I'm going to keep my eyes on him the whole class. If he tries any shit like that again, he's going to the hospital."

"No, Rick, you are not going to touch him." Then she reiterated, "Do you hear me? No touching."

"Well, what am I supposed to do, watch him molest you?"

"No, you are going to stay close by, get in the way, divert, distract and otherwise make it impossible for him to get close to me." She realized this was the first time she didn't feel angry or self-conscious with Rick. She felt like he was her anonymous pen pal friend again.

"You know, I'm not good at bamboozling," Rick said.

"Well, you did a great job befuddling me all last year," Jan said smiling at the memory of all those letters asking her to join a secret, subversive and imaginary organization.

"Okay, fine. I'll do whatever it takes to keep the physics creep from fondling you again," he said. Then with a smile back at Jan he added, "Besides, I want to be the one to fondle you."

"We'll have to talk about that later," Jan said, still smiling.

Major Stanley behaved that day and continued to keep his distance from Jan. She soon realized the bigger threat was physics itself, rather than the physics professor, when her first exam came back. One enormous red letter faced her from the front page: D.

The first month of yearling year passed quickly. Leslie wasn't able to find Angel's phone number or address from anyone in the CAS club. Jan tried calling information but she could not specify the exact "Trane" family in the greater Queens area. There were a few hundred possible options. She placed the receiver back on its hook and pulled the bi-fold doors to exit the small glass cubicle housing the only pay phone on the second floor. She returned to her room to find Kristi and Pamela waiting for her.

"Jan, have you seen the new table assignments?" Pamela asked.

"No, are they posted already?" Each company posted new table assignments every Sunday evening. Weekly rotation of the meal seating arrangements was meant to create company cohesion and bonding.

"Yeah, and what a surprise, all three of us are on the battalion diet tables," Kristi announced, rolling her eyes.

Companies ate together at tables of ten cadets each. However, some cadets, mostly women, were assigned to battalion diet tables with lower calorie meals and smaller portions. This plan might have been helpful if it didn't further separate and isolate the women from the men. Diet tables only served to stigmatize and promote the stereotype of the fat female cadet. On top of that, they did nothing to help women lose weight. In fact, they seemed to have the opposite effect.

"Goddammit," Jan groused while turning around and walking back out her door. She headed to the company bulletin board where John Heggenbach stood reading the new lists. Jan approached beside him and looked for her name. Tables 221 through 230 held the names of everyone in the company except for hers. Below the list of table assignments was written:

*Battalion DIET TABLES: Wishart

She knew that Kristi and Pamela saw the same thing on their company bulletin board.

"Did you have something to do with this, John?" Last year Jan's superiors volleyed her from diet tables to body fat testing. But plebe year was over and she was not going to allow him or anyone else to push her around anymore.

"Somehow I knew you would think that. But no, I didn't have anything to do with it."

Her nostrils involuntarily flared at the scent of his cologne or deodorant or whatever smelled pleasant. She glared into his brown eyes and noticed for the first time that one was slightly smaller than the other. She also noted he was only an inch or so taller than her. Yet he had seemed much bigger outside in formation.

"Who decided this, then? I'm tired of being singled out for diet tables when there are plenty of others in the company who need it more than I do." Jan was referring to the six or eight male cadets in G-1 who were clearly overweight. One or two were football players, but still, they were fat. *I don't buy the bullshit that they're all muscle.* Jan was all muscle, too, for that matter—except for boobs and butt—and she always weighed under the limit for her height.

"If you are within the limits of the Army height/weight tables and you are passing your PT tests, then you have a legitimate reason to protest the diet table assignment," he said.

What? Is he agreeing with me? "So you are not behind this?"

"No, I'm not." They stared at each other for another long moment. "But obviously, someone thinks you need to be on diet tables."

This was the first time Jan had an actual conversation with John. He seemed respectful at least, if not slightly kind. "Whom do you think this 'someone' might be?"

"The first sergeant makes the list each week but he likely didn't make that decision on his own. Someone else must have been involved. You should talk to him," John said.

"Okay, I will. Thank you for your help." She meant it, but it came out a little sharp, like she was being sarcastic.

"Jan, why don't you get rid of that thing?" John asked.

"What thing?"

"That chip on your shoulder," he said as he walked away.

Jan stared at his back until he disappeared, wondering how he so quickly figured out her major flaw.

"The TAC sent a memo," Cadet Paul Issacson, the G-1 first sergeant said, "ordering you on diet tables."

"Did the memo list anyone else?" Jan asked. "Cadet Cawley has got to be thirty pounds overweight, and Cadet Leif must be at least twenty." She could guesstimate their weights due to the company weigh-ins where everyone's weight was shouted out loud for all to hear.

"No, he didn't mention any other names," Issacson admitted.

"What about Cadet Lewis who failed the APRT last year? And Cadet Hamberg failed the IOCT, right?" Whoever failed PT tests was also common knowledge as the scores were publically displayed on the company bulletin boards.

"Look, you're barking up the wrong tree. I just take orders from the Captain Landau. You will need to talk to him if you have complaints," Issacson said.

"Fine, I will." *This is why I have a freaking chip on my shoulder!*

The next morning, she glanced down at her shined shoes and straight gig line before feeling the sides of her class shirt, ensuring a tight dress-off. Then she walked downstairs to the TAC's office on the first floor. She knocked twice, neither loudly nor softly.

"Enter."

"Sir, Cadet Wishart reporting to ask a question," Jan said as she saluted Captain Landau.

"What is it, Miss Wishart?" He didn't look up from the paperwork on his desk.

"Sir, I'd like to ask why I've been assigned to diet tables. I'm not over my weight limit and I've passed all my previous fitness tests." Jan felt confident that he didn't have any real reason to keep her on diet tables.

Landau kept his face down. "Most female cadets struggle with their weight, and I think you will benefit from the diet tables. You should be happy about it since the food won't be as tempting as the regular tables."

"Sir, the diet tables only serve to further alienate me from the guys. It removes me from the company tables where we get to know each other," she said.

"That seems a small price to pay. Besides the answer is simple—lose some weight and you can go back to the company tables."

"But sir, I am not overweight. I fall within the acceptable range for my height," Jan protested.

"You are at the high end of the chart. This is a preventative action—for your own good, Miss Wishart." Landau finally looked up.

"Sir, it's embarrassing and humiliating. Also, several other male cadets in G-1 are actually overweight—but they are not assigned to diet tables." There, she said it.

Captain Landau put down his pen. He leaned back in his chair and stretched his arms out, then brought them to the back of his head. He glanced to his left, at his "wall of honor," where about twenty plaques and frames showed off his diplomas, military awards and pictures with generals. He returned his gaze to Jan. "Miss Wishart, do you really want to start off in your new company this way? Complaining? It seems to me that female cadets do an awful lot of complaining. And right now you are proving my theory."

Jan could feel her heart beat faster as a trickle of sweat ran down her back. "Sir, with all due respect, I am not complaining. I am seeking equal treatment."

Captain Landau started chuckling. Then he began laughing. Hard. He leaned forward, placing his elbows on his desk and covering his eyes with the palms of his hands. Still laughing. He laughed for what seemed like a minute while Jan continued to stand at attention in front of his desk. She heard the sound of cadet shoes walking in the hallway behind her.

"Cadet Heggenbach, come here a minute!" Captain Landau shouted as he leaned to his right and looked beyond Jan, out his office door.

Shit.

John walked into the office and stood next to Jan. "Yes, sir?"

"John, Miss Wishart wants 'equal treatment,'" Landau said, still chuckling, using his fingers like quotation marks around the last two words. "What do you think of that?"

"Sir, I am not sure what you mean?" John said with a serious face.

"She's complaining about being on diet tables and wants 'equal treatment,'" Landau said, again using his fingers to make quotations again.

Jan felt her neck and face go red, yet she decided to try once more. "Sir, I just don't think it's fair to single me out for the diet tables when there are at least half a dozen men in G-1 who are overweight."

Captain Landau sat upright in his chair and placed his hands, palms down on his desk. He was not chuckling anymore. "Miss Wishart, when females can do as many pushups as men, when females can run as fast as men, when females can carry fifty pounds on their backs for miles at a time, THEN you can talk to me about 'equal treatment.' But until that time, I don't give a goddamn shit what you think about being on diet tables or anything else. You got me, Sunshine?"

She hesitated a moment. "Yes, sir." She knew she would never again come to Captain Landau for anything.

"Good. Now get the hell out of my office."

She saluted, executed an about face, and marched out the door.

She heard John following but since she was close to tears, she kept walking quickly down the hallway. She broke into a run at the stairwell, taking the steps two at a time, then she ran down the second floor hallway until she arrived at her room. Myrna was not there. She sat on her bed, lifted her hands on her face and burst into tears.

When she opened her eyes, she saw the lower half of gray trousers, ending in black cadet shoes, about a foot away from her knees. She shot her head up to see John Heggenbach standing there. "Don't sneak up on me like that!" she protested while standing up.

"I thought you heard me come in," he said.

"Well, I didn't." She was embarrassed that he had seen her crying. She had always made sure never to cry in front of male cadets—ever. "What do you want, Cadet Heggenbach?" They were about two feet apart, John only slightly taller than Jan.

"I wanted to say I'm sorry Captain Landau spoke to you like that." He looked straight into her eyes. "You are right. It's not fair that he singled you out to be on diet tables when there are several guys who deserve it more."

Jan couldn't think of anything to say.

"So I just wanted you to know that, um, I agree with you on this." He suddenly seemed embarrassed about something.

"Okay," Jan said, "thanks." She looked down at her hands.

John took a small step closer to Jan. Once again, she smelled his cologne or deodorant or whatever was sweetly emanating from his skin. "Listen, you have two options," he said. "You can just accept it and go to the diet tables like a good cadet. Or you can get a body fat test from DPE and they will send the results to Captain Landau with a recommendation. If you are under twenty percent, the TAC cannot keep you on the diet tables. But if you are over, then he can keep you on them as long as he wants."

She and Kristi had to get BFTs last year. It involved strapping on a harness and being lowered into the pool. Jan didn't exactly relish the idea of doing that again. She was pretty sure Kristi would rather stay on diet tables than have to do another BFT.

John was still standing in her personal space, and she couldn't decide whether she liked that or not. "Uh, okay," she said.

He seemed to sense her hesitation and stepped back again. "I'd get the BFT if I were you. You are very likely to be under twenty percent."

"Oh, okay." They stared at each other for another awkward moment before John turned and walked out the door.

EIGHT

"If you don't have my Army supplied, and keep it supplied, we'll eat your mules up, sir."
(William Tecumseh Sherman, USMA Class of 1840)

September 22, 1982
1530 hours

She turned the knob of her small mailbox, number 656, in the Cadet Post Office located in the basement of Washington Hall. The first letter from Drew had arrived. She tore it open on her way to Team Handball practice.

Dear Jan,

I hope this letter finds you in good health and good spirits. I have recently moved to the "Big Apple," only a short distance away from your digs on the Hudson. Hopefully you will be able to visit me sometime. I'd love to see you and hear all about the latest gossip at Woo Poo U.

I'm apprenticing as assistant staff reporter at The New York Times *(ironic, I know.) It's a great opportunity for me while I figure out what I want to do for the rest of my life. I have a small flat that I'm sharing with a guy from the Bronx. We get along well.*

I can't say I miss West Point. In fact, I'm beginning to realize that being kicked out was probably for the best. It was devastating at first, of course, but I have come to see it more as a gift. I would not have left on my own and I really needed to leave. I can tell you more when we meet in person.

I was shocked to hear what happened to you and Kristi after I left last year. I had to drive fifty miles to Birmingham to get a copy of The New York Times *to read the full story as my hometown paper doesn't cover anything more than the annual United Methodist Church's bake sale. My cousin, a GS-13 in Washington, DC, was able to send me a little more information. I had no idea that you and Kristi were involved until I received your letter a few weeks ago.*

My God, woman! I am so thankful you are okay and that you and Kristi have been cleared of all charges. Still! Please be more careful, will you?

That brings me to the only thing I miss about being at the university on the Hudson: you. All the good memories I have of USMA involve you. I mean it, Jan. You made it fun. And if the only thing I ever keep from that place is your friendship, then it will have been worth every goddamn, shitty thing that happened.

I hope you'll come visit me when you can. You understand why I can't visit you, right?

Please write back. I know you're busy, but make a little time for me, would you?

Love, Drew

Yes, Drew, I will definitely visit you in the city. And I'll visit Angel too and find out why the hell she left.

Jan held the letter tightly as she ran the rest of the way to Arvin Gymnasium.

Jan and Kristi finished their walking tours by late September. Along with Pamela, they celebrated by going to the next home football game and making the rounds at various pre- and post-game tailgate parties. Being a female cadet did have its advantages; one was being asked to join almost every tailgate they encountered. The rarity of West Point women gave them semi-celebrity status. Old grads and Army enthusiasts seemed eager to meet the female cadets and share their beer with them. None of these weekend visitors knew about Jan and Kristi's past. At tailgates, they were simply two female cadets who looked like they could use a few beers. And that was the only drawback to these free Saturday parties—drinking way too much, which tended to lead to other vices.

The sun began setting as they lingered at the last tailgate of the day. A couple of '69 grads had set their command post on the back of two pickup trucks. An old army blanket draped across a table holding various dishes: macaroni salad, chips and dip, hot dog and hamburger buns, ketchup, mustard, homemade cookies and a bowl of red grapes. A smoking grill held several burgers and dogs, which the old grads doled out to the newest guests: Pamela, Kristi and Jan, all three of whom had already been to three or four tailgates, having at least one beer at each stop.

When the friends finished eating, one of the old grads hoisted his beer and toasted the already toasty women. "Here's to all you female fadets," he slurred. "Wish you had been here back in our day. It would have made things much more," he hiccupped, "in-fresting."

The assembly including their wives and various friends raised their beers and cheered, "Hear, hear," "Hell, yeah," or other affirmation.

After everyone took a gulp, Kristi offered her own toast. "And here's to the old grads who can 'preciate a good thing when they see it." The group laughed and guzzled more beer.

Then Pamela raised a toast. "To all our sisters in cadet gray, may we live long and prosper!"

"Hear, hear," "Shit, ya," "Salute!"

Jan figured it was her turn. She raised her beer. "To weekly weigh-ins, diet tables and Body Fat Tests!"

"Hear, hear," "Shit, ya," "Salute!"

"One more," Jan was on a roll. "To professors who rub their dicks against our asses—and anyone else who tries to screw with us—they can all go to hell!"

Nothing. No lifted beers. No cheering. No gulping.

What the hell did I just say? She had to stop drinking. Whatever she just said, it must have been a huge blunder. *Dammit. Not again.*

"Ummm...." Jan tried to recover. "Did I really just say that?" She started chuckling. "I can't believe I just said that...." She kept laughing, hoping they would realize it was the libations talking.

Pamela chuckled too. "No more beer for Jan."

Kristi chimed in, "That's our Jan! She always has a way with words."

"Does that really happen?" One of the '69 grads asked.

"What?" Jan acted like she had no idea what he meant.

"Do professors really rub themselves against your butt?"

"Well," Jan looked to Kristi and Pamela for help. She couldn't lie. Yet she didn't want to be entirely truthful. "It's happened at least once that I know of," she said.

"But it's not like, a regular thing, is it?" The old grad seemed incredulous.

"No, no, I don't think so." Jan replied knowing at least ten women who had something similar happen with a professor or a TAC, a classmate or an upperclassman, or someone else in uniform.

The atmosphere had taken a downward turn. Instead of jesting and toasting, they had started a serious conversation. *Way to go, Jan.*

"I wonder if that's why so many women have resigned," the old grad's wife said.

Jan, Pamela and Kristi looked at each other. They had heard of a few resignations, but not "so many."

"How many have resigned?" Pamela asked the woman.

The woman looked at her husband before saying, "Our friends' daughter resigned last week. She told her parents that fifteen women in her class left in September alone."

"All plebes?" Kristi asked.

"Yes. She had made it through Beast and her parents thought the worst was over. Then, just like that," the woman snapped her fingers, "she called to tell them she's quitting."

"What reason did she give?" Jan asked.

The old grad spoke. "She was vague about it. She just said it wasn't for her anymore. Which totally perplexed her parents, who said she had been 'gung-ho' until that point."

Jan began to wonder how many of her classmates had left since plebe year. She had heard of a few including Angel, who had resigned at the end of Camp Buckner. She had not heard about anyone else leaving since then.

Pamela said, "We're sorry to hear that, but not really surprised."

Jan shot her a look and asked, "We're not?"

"It's not exactly like going to the University of Miami." Kristi added. "Or Ohio State or Auburn or UCLA."

"Well, that's for damn sure." The other old grad raised his beer. "Here's to the cadet women like you who have balls of steel."

His wife elbowed him. "Larry, that's not nice."

"Oh yes it is, ma'am," Kristi protested. "You have no idea how nice that is." They all started laughing again.

NINE

"An Army is a team. It lives, sleeps, eats, and fights as a team. This individual heroic stuff is pure horse shit."
(General George S. Patton, USMA Class of 1909)

October 2, 1982
0015 hours

Jan changed into her USMA sweatshirt and sweatpants before climbing under her Gray Girl. She waited for three things to happen: Taps playing on the Corps-wide speakers; the CQ opening their door asking, "All right?" to which Jan and Myrna replied, "All right;" and Myrna's breathing becoming deep and steady, revealing she was asleep. It was then that Jan quietly rose and tiptoed to the door. She made sure her card was in the "unmarked" position before leaving the room.

A plastic card with their cadet ID photo hung just inside the door to their rooms. They were required to mark their card whenever they left their rooms. If they went to the bathroom, the computer room, the library or another cadet room, they moved the marker to "academic." The card could be marked "leave" or "Post" if a cadet was authorized those luxuries, or "Athletics" for when cadets were at their sporting requirements.

Every two hours and at Taps, a yearling Charge of Quarters (CQ) came by each room, opened the door and asked, "all right?" This universal question meant, "Have you been where you marked your card?" Everyone in the room usually replied, "all right." If cadets went somewhere "illegal," they were supposed to fess up and say, "NOT all right, sir." Jan wondered why anyone would do that since it defeated the purpose of *sneaking* out. Yet if you said "all right" after going beyond the limits of the card indicator, it could be an Honor violation.

Fortunately, everyone knew about the loophole, which was simply to leave the card in the "unmarked" position. That way, cadets could still break the rules without breaking the Honor Code.

She snuck down the hallway, down two sets of stairs until she came to the basement hallway, where the three company dayrooms and storage rooms were located. She tiptoed to the G-1 dayroom, slipped inside and quickly closed the door behind her. It was completely dark.

"Jan, is that you?" he asked.

"What would you do if it wasn't?" She felt her way around one row of old mustard-colored couches. Three rows of four couches faced a television mounted high up on the opposite wall.

"Then I'd make the best of whoever came in," he said as he reached out and grabbed her. They started laughing and kissing as they fell down on the middle couch in the middle row.

After the last tailgate, Jan, Kristi and Pamela made their way to Eisenhower Hall where they bought and consumed another pitcher of beer. They also split a pizza, and that's when Rick Davidson and three others from their battalion swooped in. The four guys pushed into their booth until the three women were squished next to each other with no way to escape except by climbing under or over the table. The trio didn't mind though. It always felt good when the guys socialized with them. Rick had been scrunched on Jan's right, putting them in physical contact for the first time. Being drunk made it all too easy for both of them to flirt.

It started when Rick placed his hand on Jan's leg. She reached down and covered his hand with hers. Amidst the talking and laughing, Rick rubbed her leg that was covered by her dress gray trousers. She moved her hand onto his leg and did the same. There was no indication above the table as to what was going on below the table.

On the walk back to the barracks, Jan and Rick diverted behind the mess hall. They stopped a few times in the darkness of the loading docks and kissed passionately. It was dangerously close to Taps when they were supposed to be in their rooms for the night. So they made a plan to meet in the G-1 company dayroom shortly after the bedtime bell and after the CQ had made the rounds to every room.

Jan had made up her mind while she waited under her Gray Girl. She was going to do it. Tonight. With Rick Davidson. She would lose her virginity tonight. Jan wanted to find out what everyone else seemed to already know about sex. Regan, her best friend from high school, made it seem like the second *Great Awakening*. Kristi had told her how awesome it could be. So Jan wanted in on the secret.

Let's see what all the fuss is about. She also figured Rick would be the best guy to show her whatever it was she was missing.

Rick already had his hands under her USMA sweatshirt. She purposely left her bra behind to help speed up the process. She had to admit that she liked Rick Davidson's hands on her breasts. She felt a tingling sensation in her thighs. He lifted her sweatshirt and began licking or sucking (she wasn't sure which, maybe both) her nipples. She liked that very much.

She didn't quite know what to do with her hands at this point. She had them on Rick's back, then moved them to his head, then back to his back. She knew at some point she would need to move them somewhere else, but she figured she'd let him take the lead on all those decisions.

Then it happened. Rick began pulling down her sweatpants. *Oh shit, oh shit, oh shit.* She purposely left her underpants behind for the same reason—to hasten the process. Now, she wished she had kept on one more layer. The sweatpants were somewhere at knee level. She felt his erection throbbing to get in. She hadn't even had to touch him there. *Well, that was easy.*

This was it. *The* moment. The one everyone had talked about except her because she hadn't done it before. But now, she would finally experience it. She would soon be a member of "The Club." And she would finally be clued in to the big secret that was sex.

Except at the very moment, when Rick was about to insert his penis into Jan's vagina (which is the exact wording Jan remembered from her seventh grade human reproduction class), the dayroom door flung open.

They froze.

"Get in here, woman!" The male voice whisper-shouted.

"Owww, that hurts," the female voice cracked.

Jan felt Rick deflate. They heard muffled giggling and some scuffling. It seemed as though the man had pushed the woman into the dayroom and was now leaning her over one of the couches. Jan couldn't tell whether it was playful or not while she kept thinking about her sweatpants being below her crotch.

"Ouch, stop it, Joey!" Jan recognized Violet Carpetta's voice.

"Oh c'mon, baby, you know you like it," he said. Jan thought maybe he twisted her arm or pulled her hair, or something like that. "Now, let's get down to it, baby." They heard a thud.

Did he just push Violet to the floor?

"Wait!" she pleaded.

Jan and Rick had already begun cinching up their sweatpants. Neither made a sound as they reassembled themselves.

"Wait for what, Vy?" the male voice asked. "What are we waiting for?"

They heard her whine, "I just don't feel like it tonight, Joey..."

"Oh, come on, baby...don't do that to me, again..."

Rick jumped up first, followed immediately by Jan, who shouted, "If she doesn't feel like it, then leave her the fuck alone!"

Rick ran to turn on the lights. They squinted from the harsh brightness. Violet's boyfriend, a firstie named Joey Leshiski, looked stunned. "What the hell are you two doing down here?"

"We were enjoying each other's company, asshole," Rick said, "until you interrupted us." Jan loved it when Rick acted like this—like someone who didn't fear upperclassmen. "And we're all breaking the same rules right now, so don't pretend we're the only ones in trouble here."

"Actually, Rick," Jan added, "we were here by choice, so Joey's breaking one more rule than us."

"That's right," Rick said, then added, "Joey, you always shove your girlfriend around like that?"

"It's none of your business," Joey protested.

"Yes, yes it is. We didn't walk in on you, remember, you walked in on us." Rick argued.

"In *my company* dayroom, mind you. And we heard everything you said and did to Violet." Jan nodded to Violet, who was now standing next to Joey.

The firstie shifted his weight from one foot to the other. He had been caught. And the two yearlings were not afraid to tell what they had heard. He could not deny it without violating the Honor Code. He was trapped.

"Let's all just go back to our rooms now," Violet finally spoke.

What??

"What Joey and I do together is our own business. Just like whatever you two were doing is your business. So let's just leave it at that," Violet said softly but firmly.

You're an idiot! "Violet, a minute ago you were pleading for Joey to stop hurting you. No one deserves to be treated like that," Jan said.

Violet gave Joey a look that said, *I'll handle this*. "Jan, we have our way of doing things and you have your way of doing things. Let's all just go back to our rooms."

Is she inferring that they were "role playing?" Was that "rough talk" just part of their fun? Jan remembered seeing bruises on Violet's arms and legs before. Maybe it was something she liked, although it sure didn't sound like Violet had liked it earlier. Jan couldn't imagine how anyone enjoyed being abused.

"Wait, Violet, just so I'm clear, are you saying you want us to ignore the fact that Joey was hurting you?" Jan asked.

"Joey wasn't hurting me. We have a...unique relationship."

"Okay, Violet. Whatever you say." Jan shook her head. "I hope I never have a 'unique relationship' like yours."

Jan tiptoed into her room. She slid under her Gray Girl without removing her clothes.

"Where were you?"

Myrna's question startled Jan. "Um, I just came back from the bathroom." It was true. Jan had stopped at the bathroom right before coming back to the room.

"You've been gone for over an hour."

What? Are you my mother? Jan knew she had to tell the truth or face another Honor Code violation. "I went to the dayroom."

"What for?"

It was pointless to lie or even argue. "I met a guy there. But before we could do anything we were interrupted by another couple."

"Who?"

"Who, what?"

"Who was the guy and who was the other couple?"

"I'd rather not say, Myrna. I don't want to get anyone else in trouble."

"Jan, I'm not going to rat on you. I'm just curious who you were with."

"You promise you won't tell anyone else?" Jan asked.

"Promise."

"Okay. I met Rick Davidson in the dayroom. Then Violet Carpetta and Joey Lishiski showed up."

"Mmmm."

"Mmmm, what?"

"Nothing. I was just thinking, that's all."

"Thinking about what, Myrna? C'mon, I just told you what you wanted to know, you can at least tell me what you're thinking."

"Well, I was just thinking that Rick Davidson is not your type. And Joey Lishiski is definitely not the right person for Violet."

Jan didn't like Myrna's know-it-all attitude. She thought Myrna was the worst person to make a judgment about heterosexual relationships. "Well, I happen to like Rick Davidson. A lot. He was a good friend to me last year and our relationship has grown since then."

"Whatever, Jan. It's your life. I just think he's all wrong for you."

Whatever, Myrna. As if I give a shit what you think. "You're right about Violet and Joey, though." Then, because she didn't want to elaborate she said, "Goodnight, Myrna."

"Night, Jan."

Before drifting to sleep, Jan revisited the events since Taps. Her plans to be "deflowered" had been thwarted by Violet and Joey, which pissed her off at first. Then she began to realize their intrusion might have been one of those divine interventions Rick used to write about. Instead of being angry, she felt deeply thankful their rash encounter had been abruptly halted.

Geez. What an idiot I am.

She decided right then to make that appointment first thing Monday morning—for birth control pills.

TEN

"If you are going through hell, keep going."
(Winston Churchill)

October 6, 1982
1730 hours

Jan glanced over at Rick Davidson on the men's side of the court. They hadn't spoken to each other since their "almost sex" in the dayroom. If both coaches dismissed the teams at the same time, she would try to time it so they could walk back to the barracks together.

The Team Handball team ran through the usual dribbling, passing and shooting drills. Four new plebes kept dribbling the ball too long and then planting a foot while holding the ball, as in basketball, instead of taking the allowed three steps. These were common errors among ex-basketball players who had the skill set, but not the feel for the game yet.

When practice ended Captain Hasuko reviewed the logistics for their upcoming tournament in Montreal. "Report to Central Area at 1530 hours on Friday to load the bus. Uniform is dress gray, you can remove your coats once on the bus. Only one bag allowed per person."

The men's team had been dismissed. Some of the guys, including Rick Davidson, stayed behind to pick up the stray balls. *C'mon Hasuko...dismiss us!*

"Make sure you have both pairs of team uniforms. There will be two matches on Saturday and one on Sunday. Curfew will be strictly enforced," Coach continued.

Jan saw Rick put the last ball away and start to walk off the court. *Let's go, let's go!*

"I know everyone likes to have fun on these trips," Hasuko continued. "But I want you to remember we are playing in a tournament. That's the main priority. Does everyone understand?"

Yes, yes, we do.

"Okay, good," Coach said. "Any questions before you go?"

No, no, no one has any! Rick was well on his way down the six flights of stairs.

"Yes, Miss Juanez?"

Damn beanhead! Jan would never have asked a question when she was a new plebe on the team.

"Sir, will we need civilian clothes for the trip?" Juanez asked.

Oh, geez, what a dweeb.

"Unless you want to wear dress gray when you go out after the matches," Captain Hasuko said with a smile. "All right, if there's nothing more, you are dismissed."

Finally! Jan stood and began to bolt out the door.

"Miss Wishart," Captain Hasuko called before she reached the stairway. "I need to speak with you a moment."

Ahhhhhhhh! Of course you do. "Yes, sir." She walked back to the bleacher side of the court.

"Come sit down, will you?" Coach said with a serious face.

Uh-oh, what'd I do? Jan sat on the bottom bleacher while Captain Hasuko remained standing.

"You were Angel Trane's roommate last year weren't you?" he asked.

"Yes, sir." She could not even imagine where this was heading.

"Well, as you know, she resigned over the summer. I'm not at liberty to say why, but I serve on a special panel, appointed by the Secretary of the Army. We are looking into, among other things, the circumstances surrounding her decision to leave." Captain Hasuko said. "Our panel is meeting next month, the same weekend as our tournament in DC."

Okay, why are you telling me this?

"Miss Trane will also be there. She asked to see you while we are there. I told her we would find a time that works for all of us to meet. Are you okay with that?"

Jan thought she misheard him. "Did you say Angel is going to be in DC the same weekend as our tournament?" Captain Hasuko nodded his head up and down. "And she wants to meet with me?" Coach nodded again. "I've been trying to get a hold of her, why didn't she write or call me?"

"I don't know, but she specifically asked me to talk with you. The panel is meeting between the first and second match on Saturday. You can go with me and see Miss Trane then."

"Okay, yes, of course, I want to see her. But why is your panel looking into her resignation?"

"I can't tell you that."

"Can you give me her phone number, sir?" Jan asked.

"I'd rather not do that without her permission. She will explain everything when you see her." Coach sounded a little sad.

"Okay, sir. I'm just glad to finally hear something about her. If you speak to her before then, please tell her I can't wait to see her." Jan decided this news was worth missing the walk back with Rick.

"Will do. Uh, Jan," Coach said, using her first name, "this needs to remain between us. I mean about the panel and all."

"Yes, sir." Jan felt a slight headache coming on.

G, H and I companies fell in for dinner formation on the New South pavement. Jan decided she would catch up with Rick once inside the mess hall to say "hi," or "see you this weekend," or "when can we go to the dayroom again?" It always seemed much harder to communicate when alcohol wasn't involved.

She passed several I-1 tables on her way to the battalion diet tables and saw Rick taking off his gray overcoat and wrapping it over the back of his chair. She walked directly toward him, gray saucer cap in hand and unbuttoning her gray coat. She could tell he saw her, too. How could he not see her? She smiled and nodded while closing the distance between them. She opened her mouth to say the rehearsed line. *Let's sit together on the bus to Montreal.* But the words never left her tongue.

Within a few feet of him, Rick abruptly turned away from her and walked toward a company mate at the next table. Jan stopped short. It was an obvious snub. He deliberately cut her off just as she was about to speak to him.

Message received. Jan closed her mouth. *Regroup. Remain calm.* She executed a half turn, as if she meant to go through that particular row of tables, and continued weaving around more tables until she reached the battalion diet table. *Carry on.*

"They did it again," Kristi whispered as they sat down.

"What?"

"Someone sliced my textbooks. They're all ruined. I have to buy new ones."

"Jesus, Kissy. This has got to stop. Let's go talk to your company commander after dinner."

Across the table, Pamela said, "We've already done that."

"And? What did he say?" Jan asked.

"He said he would make a company-wide announcement that anyone caught vandalizing property will receive an automatic slug," Pamela said.

"That's it?"

Kristi said, "He doesn't think there's anything else he can do."

"Okay, let's talk to your TAC tomorrow morning, then," Jan insisted.

"He's not going to help much either," Pamela said. "He's already told Kristi that she better not cause any 'problems' for him."

"This is shit!" Jan shouted. The diet table commander, a woman from I-1, furrowed her brow at Jan.

"Everything all right down there?" the I-1 firstie asked.

"Well, actually," Pamela spoke up, "we have a problem you might be able to help us with."

"What is it?"

"What would you do if, say for instance, someone left a dead snake on your bed, pissed in your shoes and cut up all your textbooks?" Pamela asked.

"Is that really happening?" the table commander asked.

"Yes," Jan stated.

"That's serious stuff, you need to report it to the MPs," the woman stated. "Go through the chain of command first, though. Speak to your CO and your TAC, but if they don't take action, then report it to the MPs."

They hadn't even thought about involving the MPs. No one ever called in the MPs—that just wasn't done. Ever.

"Are we allowed to do that?" Jan asked.

"If a crime has been committed, then yes," she answered.

"But is this a crime or a prank?" Kristi asked.

"Well, I'd say the first two could be pranks, but cutting up your textbooks is a crime, I believe."

"Kissy," Jan said, "if we involve the MPs at this point, we're just asking for more trouble. Why don't you see if you can talk to the commandant first? You know, use your connections." Jan widened her eyes referring to the fact that Kristi's father was the ambassador to Germany.

"Okay, I'll start there," Kristi said. "But if this shit keeps up, I'm calling the MPs."

"Great," Jan sighed. "Just what we need—more MP investigations."

They all knew what she meant. After "the incident" last year, there was an extensive MP investigation. Both Jan and Kristi were exonerated, of course, but they wanted another MP investigation about as much as they wanted a gynecological exam.

ELEVEN

"Military power wins battles, but spiritual power wins wars."
(General George Marshall, VMI Class of 1901)

October 15, 1982
1900 hours

She jerked awake just as the West Point gates diminished from the bus window. She must have fallen asleep while waiting for the others to load the bus. Her anxiety level dropped with each passing mile. It would only be temporary, but at least for a couple of days while on the Team Handball trip to Montreal, she could relax a little.

Jan spoke briefly with Caroline, a bubbly classmate with a hyena-like laugh, who spent almost the entire ride flirting with several guys on the men's team. On one hand, Jan wished she could be more like Caroline and socialize easily, especially with guys. *On the other hand, I'm happy I don't have her cackle.*

After eight long hours, they finally arrived at the hotel, unloaded their bags and fanned out to their assigned rooms. Jan, Caroline, Pepper and another cow, Annette, shared one room with two queen beds, which was standard fare for Team Handball trips.

After settling in, everyone changed into civvies and most of both teams walked to the nearest bar. Jan hoped she would find an opportunity to talk with Rick. Drinking always made that process easier and she felt sure they would reconnect that night.

Seven cadets smashed together into a booth and ordered pitchers of beer, another standard fare of Team Handball trips. Jan sat between Caroline and another yearling on the team, Carrie, whose laughter sounded almost exactly like Caroline's. Two cow guys sat on Carrie's side, while two yearlings, Rick and Wade, sat on Caroline's side. Jan noted she was the middle person in the booth with the worst vantage point for talking to any of the guys.

Great, I've managed to get the best seat in the house, between the two hyenas.

The "two C's," as Jan began to think of them, continued to irritate her. But since she was trapped between them, she decided to just keep drinking. This was her one consolation as Caroline became increasingly cozy with Rick.

At long last, someone mentioned the curfew. Jan was thrilled at the chance to escape the twittering birds. She was drunk, too, as they all had become by then. They settled up the bar tab and stumbled out of the door for the short, cold walk to the hotel.

The "two C's" needed help walking and Rick offered his arm to Caroline. Jan, walking completely unaided, almost fell over when they started kissing.

That's it! I'm done with him. She ran the rest of the way back to the hotel.

Annette and Pepper sat pretzel style on one queen bed. Jan nodded to them when she came in the door. She headed straight to the bathroom, changed into pajamas, washed her face and brushed her teeth. She climbed into the remaining bed and slid under the covers, not wanting to think about having to eventually share it with Caroline.

"Was it fun?" Pepper asked.

"Yeah, it was okay," Jan said.

"Where's Caroline?" Annette inquired.

"Not sure...she was making out with...someone." Jan didn't see any reason to pretend otherwise but decided to change the focus anyway. "What did you guys do?"

"We ordered pizza and just stayed in and talked."

They could do that much at West Point, for crying out loud. "Why didn't you go out with the rest of us?"

Pepper replied, "We just don't like that whole bar scene. Besides, we were so blessed by staying here in the Word."

What the hell is she talking about? Jan had no idea what Pepper meant until she lifted her head and noticed for the first time that a Bible was open on their bed. *Oh God, I'm rooming with a drunken hyena and a couple of religious fanatics!* "Wow, that's awesome."

"We were just about to have prayer. Would you like to join us?" Annette asked.

Oh man, you've got to be kidding me. What's wrong with these people? "Okay," Jan complied and sat up. The two women held each other's hand and reached over to grab Jan's hands. *Oh no, not the dreaded hand hold too!*

"Dear Father," Pepper began, "we thank you for this day, for the chance to be here with our brothers and sisters to play Team Handball and fellowship together. We thank you for the opportunity to share your love, your grace, your peace in whatever ways we can. Thank you for our teammates, especially Jan and Caroline, whom you have placed with us this weekend. Please watch over Caroline and bring her safely back to this room. And give Jan your help, in whatever ways she might need it."

Oh Lord, when's this gonna end?

"Gracious Lord, you have always been with us, even when we didn't always know it. And we know that you are working right now, in the lives of many who need you tonight."

Can we wrap it up now? Please?

"Lord, continue to work in us, through us, and for us, so we can continue to do your work in the world."

Amen?

"Where there is darkness, bring light. Where there is suffering, bring relief. Where there is war, bring peace..."

Where there is prayer, bring it to an end.

"And where there is confusion, bring clarity. In Jesus name, we pray."

"Amen," Jan blurted out. But Annette and Pepper kept their heads down. Then Annette started to pray.

Oh God, not more...

"Lord...." Annette prayed for another few minutes. All the while Jan made comments to herself in between sentences. Finally Annette finished, and Jan thrilled at the thought that she could soon go to sleep. But when Annette announced, "In Jesus' name," they continued to keep their heads bowed. Jan wondered what was going on. Then she felt Annette and Pepper both give each of her hands a slight squeeze.

Oh no, they don't want me to pray, do they? Shit. I don't pray for God's sake!

"Ah Lord," she heard herself say, "thanks for this prayer time. Um, I really got a lot out of it. Give us each a good night's rest...ah, so we can kick some ass tomorrow. Amen."

"Amen," the other two echoed.

Jan slid back under the covers and feigned falling asleep. But three thoughts kept running through her head. One: She wished Kristi and Pamela were with her to laugh hysterically about all this. Two: How the hell were these two women more interested in God than drinking and socializing with guys? And three: What the hell were Caroline and Rick doing?

Jan raced upstairs to tell Kristi and Pamela about her weekend. Other than Violet, Joey and Myrna, they were the only others who knew about her near miss with Rick in the dayroom. *Or was it a near hit? Probably both. A miss-hit.*

"So, when did Caroline return to the room?" Pamela asked.

"I'm not sure. I fell asleep. I think it was at least a couple of hours later though." Jan felt slightly sick just thinking about it.

"Oh, then they did it for sure," Kristi said.

"Thanks, Kristi. Just what I needed to hear."

"You have to be realistic, Jan. He's a guy. This is what guys do. They screw around. A lot." Sometimes Kristi's bluntness wasn't helpful, Jan thought.

"Well, Jan," Pamela interrupted, "if you really want to know, ask Caroline."

"I did ask her, first thing the next morning. She said they didn't do anything. Just kissing. They didn't have anywhere they could go, apparently. All the rooms had three other people in them. No dayrooms to hide in either."

"Oh, come on, Jan. You didn't fall for that one, did you?" Kristi was at it again. "There's always somewhere to go. I'm sure she just didn't want to admit it to you." Kristi seemed to be an authority on these things. "And there's a good chance Rick asked her not to tell you."

Jan still held out hope. "That would mean Caroline lied, then. I don't think she would risk violating the Honor Code for that. She would have just said, 'none of your business,' or 'I'm not going to answer that,' or something else that wouldn't involve a lie."

Pamela chimed in, "She might not have remembered if she was really dunk."

"We were all drunk, but not *that* drunk," Jan said.

The conversation ended abruptly when Violet entered the room. She had just returned from the library.

Jan thought she looked remarkably changed. She had "puffed out," literally. The spaghetti arms were gone. Replaced with slightly chubby ones. Her dress gray, which draped off her before, looked almost snug. Her previously narrow face had filled in, looking fuller and rounder.

"Hey, Violet," Jan greeted her. "How's it going?"

"Hey, Jan. Fine, thanks." Violet proceeded to her desk, placing down her armload of books.

"You still seeing Joey, Violet?" Jan asked.

"Yes, Jan, I am." She sounded angry. "What about you? You still with that guy?"

"No," Jan wished she could have answered differently. "It didn't last."

"Sorry to hear that," Violet now stood in front of her closet removing her dress gray. She slid the heavy wool trousers down her legs revealing several big bruises.

Jan nodded to Kristi and Pamela while moving her eyes in Violet's direction. They saw what she meant.

"Violet," Kristi led the charge, "how'd you get those bruises on your legs?"

"What bruises?" She looked down, seeming to notice them for the first time. "Oh, these?" She recovered quickly.

"Yeah, those," Pamela said.

"I'm not sure, probably from the IOCT or something." Violet donned her bathrobe without taking off her t-shirt and underwear. "Shower time," she said as she hurried out the door.

Jan returned to her "gray cell" and wrote everything from the weekend in her journal. It was still the only place she allowed her true feelings to come out.

Just got back from a Team Handball trip. We won two of our three matches. Not bad. Although, I really don't care about winning or losing, I just love to get the hell out of Dodge!

I roomed with a couple of cows and one annoying classmate. It went further south when the hyena classmate-roommate ended up sleeping with Rick (presumed.) Then it got even worse when I returned to my room to find the two cows reading the Bible. They even got me to pray with them. It's not that I have anything against the Bible or praying, I just don't see how that could possibly be better than going out and drinking with guys. Maybe they're lesbians?

I'm all for having faith. I like to think I have faith. I believe in God. I pray. But wasn't the Bible written like thousands of years ago? Entirely by men? So even though I'm not sure what's in it, it doesn't seem to be anything I would want to read—ever!!

TWELVE

"Dripping water hollows out stone, not through force but through persistence."
(Ovid)

October 20, 1982
1525 hours

Kristi sat in a padded fabric chair with wooden arms and legs. It was one of five identical chairs lined up against the wall facing the open door of the dark and empty commandant's office. She had made an appointment to see the man behind door number two, the commandant's assistant. She could have met with the head honcho himself but she didn't want to take *that much* advantage of her unique situation. *It's good to have connections,* she thought, while Pamela Pearson leafed through the latest West Point magazine in the chair next to her. Kristi brought her along as a witness. *Just in case.*

They heard LTC Cunningham shouting behind his closed door, "I don't give a rat's ass what he said. You make damn sure she doesn't show up. I don't want her name or face anywhere near that thing, you got it?" A pause indicated a phone conversation. "Just make it happen, Benjamin, I don't care how, just do it!" He slammed the receiver down. They heard him shuffle papers and cough once. The he opened his door and took a step out of his office like he was leaving for the day. Kristi and Pamela stood up.

"Oh." LTC Cunningham seemed surprised. "How long have you been waiting?" His figure almost filled the doorway. At 6'2", two-hundred-and-fifty pounds, his physique still reflected his Army football days.

"Just a minute or two, sir," Kristi replied.

"Well, Miss McCarron, I had almost forgotten you had made an appointment. Come in, won't you?" He seemed delighted to see her. She was somewhat of a famous cadet and not just because her father was the ambassador to Germany. "I have to be at the superintendent's office in just a few minutes. I hope you understand this will have to be brief." He stepped back into his office, walked behind his desk and sat down in a large leather chair.

Kristi and Pamela stood at attention facing his desk. "Yes, sir. Sir, this is my roommate, Cadet Pearson."

"Yes, very well, what can I do for you Miss McCarron?"

Kristi continued, "sir, I've been receiving threats since the beginning of the academic year. The first week back on Post, I found a dead snake in my bed. Then someone urinated in my shoes. Most recently, I found my textbooks had been slashed. They all had to be replaced."

"I see." He looked stern. "I'm very sorry to hear that."

"Thank you, sir."

"Do you have any idea who's behind all this? It must be someone in your company, right?"

"Well, sir, it could be anyone. And it could be more than one person."

"Hmmm." He leaned back in his chair and looked over their heads as if in thought. "Have you told your CO and your TAC?"

"Sir, I told the CO, but there's not much he can do. I haven't spoken to my TAC, sir."

"Why not?"

"Sir, the first time he met me, he said I better not cause any problems for him. Doesn't make me think he will be very helpful in this case."

LTC Cunningham leaned forward. "I'm sure he didn't mean that negatively. You still need to let him know what's going on."

"Yes, sir."

"Well, I'm sure your TAC will be able to handle the situation. You let me know, of course, if there's anything else I can do." He stood up.

"Sir, if these are crimes, shouldn't the MPs be involved?" Pamela asked quickly.

"I don't think there will be any need for that, Miss...Pearson, is it?" LTC Cunningham sat back down in his leather chair. "This is just harmless harassment, which you have to expect given the events of last year. I'm sure this will all blow over in time."

"Sir, I'm not sure it's so harmless. It's getting pretty unnerving and it needs to stop," Kristi added.

"I understand, yes, of course. No one wants to be on the receiving end of such pranks. But if you just wait it out, Miss McCarron, and act like it doesn't bother you, I'm sure they will tire of their antics. They will realize that it's not affecting you and give up."

Pamela spoke up again, "sir, it IS affecting her and her friends. And sir, it might be illegal." She raised her voice on the last sentence.

LTC Cunningham interlocked his fingers and rested his elbows on his desk so that they made a triangle in front of his face. "Miss McCarron," he directed his gaze at Kristi, "I will speak to your TAC about it. Major Crutchfield, correct?"

"Yes, sir."

"I know it must feel unpleasant, ladies, but you do realize that some of this is to be expected. Male cadets have endured harassment all through the years, from so-called 'Blanket Parties' to 'Dumpster Diving.' This is part of cadet life."

"Sir, I think the major difference is that those things are considered fun and the culprits are known; they don't hide their identity," Pamela noted.

"There are other forms of harassment, however, that are carried out in secret. You would not be the first who've had to deal with this kind of thing. Or even the last, I'm afraid."

"Yes, sir. I still think it's wrong, sir. And someone should do something about it before it gets out of hand." Kristi said using her "ambassador's daughter" authority.

"You're right, Miss McCarron. I will make sure Major Crutchfield takes this seriously. Thank you for bringing it to my attention." He stood up again. "Now, I have a meeting to attend." LTC Cunningham walked around his desk and motioned toward the door.

"Thank you, sir," Kristi said as he escorted them out of his office.

"Good afternoon, ladies."

"Good afternoon, sir."

"Ma'am, may I speak with you a moment?" Jan asked Major Behar when Arabic class ended.

"Certainly," The major wore her jet-black hair in a tight bun on the top of her head. Her skin looked like smooth, silky caramel. Jan guesstimated her age to be about thirty-five.

Old. "Ma'am, I'm wondering if you had any information about the number of women cadets who have resigned this year and perhaps the reasons why they left."

Major Behar paused a moment. "It's funny you should ask, Miss Wishart." She sat down at her desk. "I was just in a meeting about this last week."

"Really? Was it here on Post, ma'am?"

"Yes, a few of my colleagues and I have been interested in the very same topic." She moved around some papers on her desk. "Are you planning to do anything with this information?"

"Well, ma'am, I'm just curious, really. I…I also have a friend who's interested in this information," Jan said, referring to Kristi or Pamela, not to mention Drew who happened to work at a major NY newspaper.

"I see. Hmmm." The professor seemed hesitant to say any more.

"Ma'am, we don't want to cause any trouble. We've just heard there's a disproportionate number of women leaving this year and we'd like to know why."

"Well, Miss Wishart, trouble is what you will get when you start asking those kinds of questions."

Uh-oh, this was a mistake.

"However, the questions must be asked. And we need more people like you and your friend who are willing to ask them."

Whew.

"My colleagues and I are in the process of collecting some data. We hope to have the information in hand in the next couple of weeks. I can share it with you then, if you can wait that long."

Jan smiled at her Arabic professor. "I would be grateful to see what you come up with, ma'am."

Major Behar smiled back. "But you must be discreet, Miss Wishart."

"Yes, ma'am."

"There are some very powerful people who are trying very hard to bury this information. Those of us who try to bring it to light risk their wrath."

"Yes, ma'am."

"So we must be very careful, Miss Wishart."

"Yes, ma'am."

THIRTEEN

IKETTE, n. A girl who frequents Eisenhower Hall for the sole purpose of picking up a helpless male cadet. Impressed only by the "man in a uniform" image.
(from Glossary of Cadet Slang)

November 12, 1982
1600 hours

The teams began loading the bus for the long-awaited Team Handball trip to Washington, DC. Jan loved all trips away from West Point, but last year's DC trip had been her favorite. This time, she would have the added benefit of seeing Angel and, hopefully, finding out why she resigned.

"Once I hear her reason for leaving, directly from the pony's mouth, then I can put the whole thing to sleep," she told Kristi before heading to the bus in Central Area.

Kristi chuckled at another one of Jan's frequent mismanagement of adages. "Jan, you do realize that you give new meaning to the term 'turn of phrase.'"

"Yeah, and you love me for it, right?" Jan figured her habit of re-wording old sayings was annoying to those who didn't know her and endearing to those who did. For that reason, she didn't put forth any effort to get them right. "Come by my room Sunday night and I'll tell you what I find out," she shouted to Kristi as she exited the barracks door.

Jan threw her bag in the compartment underneath the bus and ran up the three steps to the seating area. She immediately saw Rick at a window seat about halfway back. The aisle seat beside him was vacant, but she did not want to spend the next four-and-a-half hours next to Mr. Sourpuss, so she chose the seat directly in front of him instead. That way, she figured, he could choose to speak to her if he wanted. Or not.

Jan heard the hyena laugh even before Caroline boarded the bus. *Please, sit with someone else this time.* The thought of spending the entire ride sitting next to "Miss Congeniality," who had likely slept with Rick on the last trip, almost made her want to puke.

"Hey, Jan." Caroline stopped beside her row.

Jan had been intentionally and intently staring out the window. "Oh, hey...Caroline."

"Do you mind if I sit with someone else this time?"

"Oh, no, not at all." *Relieved, actually.*

"Great." She flopped down in the seat next to Rick. "I'll be right behind you, though, if you get bored, ha, ha, ha, ha..."

Dammit. I didn't mean THAT someone else.

It was torture. Jan had to endure every word Caroline said for the entire ride to DC. The only consolation was Rick's strange quietness. He barely uttered more than a few sentences the whole time. Jan knew he wasn't the shy, retiring type. She wondered if he was trying to send a message to Caroline: "I'm not interested in you." Or maybe he was trying to send a message to Jan: "I'm not interested in Caroline." Either way, Jan felt sure his long silence on the bus was meant to actually say something.

After winning the next morning's match, Jan and Captain Hasuko entered the Ambassador Room in the State Plaza Hotel, located next door to the Georgetown Campus. She wore her team uniform under gray USMA sweatshirt and pants, which were under her black wool parka and black beanie cap. Coach gave his permission for her to wear the informal uniform since she was not part of the panel and still had to play in the afternoon match.

Jan sat in one of the many chairs lining the perimeter of the room. A long table had been set in the middle of the room with ten Army officers seated on one side. The scene reminded her of her Honor Trial last year and she swallowed the lump that had formed in her throat just thinking about that ordeal. The panel consisted of male captains and majors, with one lieutenant colonel—the "chair"—in the middle of the green suits.

Five young women entered the room and took their seats across the table from the panel. Jan recognized only one: Angel Trane, her plebe roommate.

Lieutenant Colonel Jurgensen introduced himself and the members of the panel. Then he asked each woman to state her name, former class and company. The four others reported first before Jan heard, "Angel Trane, Class of '85, Second Company, Camp Buckner, sir." Angel had spent plebe year in Company H-3 with Jan, but she resigned before moving into a new yearling company.

Then Jan listened with growing anger and sadness as each woman told her reasons for leaving West Point.

Two had been raped. They both reported it to their superiors and were promptly grilled about what they were wearing, how much they had to drink and whom they had sex with in the last few months. They never felt safe after that.

Another women woke up one night to find a man in her bed. When she screamed, he hightailed out of her room. Although her TAC pressed her for a name, she couldn't identify her assailant with certainty. Over the next few months, she received numerous threatening messages addressed to "Bitch," "Slut," "Whore," "Cunt," "Cocksucker," and "Miss Fucks-a-lot," to name a few. She finally decided she had enough of the harassment and resigned.

The fourth woman left because her TAC began pressuring her for sex when she was a yearling. She finally consented during her cow year when he threatened her with an Honor violation. Although the relationship became consensual for a time, she felt tremendously guilty and confessed the affair to her roommate, who promptly reported it to the company commander. The married TAC was quietly moved to another position on Post and she was expelled for one year. She would have been allowed to return the following year and graduate with the next class. By then, everyone knew what had happened and she decided it was best not to return.

Jan could barely hear as Angel explained her reason for leaving the Corps of Cadets. "I became pregnant," she said softly.

What?

"I met my boyfriend at Camp Buckner and we began having sex."

I can't believe it. Even Angel beat me to it.

"We were told that we had to make an appointment at Keller Army Hospital to get birth control pills, which meant waiting until we returned to West Point at the end of the summer. So condoms seemed to work fine for a while. Until they didn't."

Geez, Angel, I had no idea.

"I found out I was pregnant at the end of July. My Buckner TAC said I had to resign. I packed my things immediately and left without telling anyone goodbye. I found out later that there were other options, but by then I had already signed on the dotted line."

I still can't believe it. Rick had been right.

Angel spoke again. "I miscarried two weeks later."

LTC Jurgensen asked, "Where is your boyfriend, Miss Trane?"

"Sir, my ex-boyfriend is still there. As far as I know, he didn't have any repercussions from all this."

They never do.

After a brief period of Q & A between the panel and the five women, LTC Jurgensen thanked them for their time and told them they could leave.

"Sir, what about Cadet Wan? Wasn't she going to speak to us today also?" Captain Hasuko interrupted before anyone stood up.

"I'm not sure why Cadet Wan isn't here. She said she was planning to come."

"Sir, perhaps I could give her a call?" Hasuko suggested.

"I don't think that is necessary, captain."

"Sir, I believe her testimony is extremely important to our investigation," Captain Hasuko continued. "If I am not mistaken, she accused a high ranking officer's son..."

"Captain Hasuko, let's not speculate..."

"Sir, perhaps one of us could interview her on the phone? It could be that she couldn't..."

"That's not the mandate we've been given, captain. We work as a panel, not as individuals," LTC Jurgensen said.

"Then, sir, perhaps a few of us could arrange to meet with her..."

"Captain Hasuko, if Cadet Wan wanted to tell us something, she would have come today."

And that was the end of that.

Jan rose and followed the five women out the door before grabbing her old roommate in a fierce hug, practically cutting off the small woman's circulation.

"Jan, I'm so glad you came!" Angel had tears in her eyes. "I wasn't sure what you had heard about me..."

"I didn't hear anything, Angel. I didn't even know you left until re-orgy week, and no one else seemed to know much about what happened, either." Jan purposely left out what Rick had told her.

"I didn't have any time to say goodbye. You know they move you out pretty quickly once it's been decided," Angel said.

"I know, I remember that from when Drew left last year. But why didn't you write or call me, Angel?"

"I was so ashamed. I mean...I had committed a sin."

"Welcome to the club," Jan said feeling slightly grateful for her lapsed Catholic status.

"Jan, seriously, I felt like I had let everyone down. Myself, most of all."

"Angel, I can see why you might have felt that way, but it's ridiculous really. I mean what did you do wrong, exactly? Other than use faulty birth control?" Jan looked her roommate in the eyes. "Oh, and being female?"

"What do you mean by that?" Angel asked.

"Well, you don't see your ex-boyfriend here, do you? He's not sharing his reasons for why he had to resign from West Point."

Angel laughed in that petite way that was so familiar and endearing to Jan. "You can still make me laugh, Jan."

"Angel, what did you mean when you said you found out later that there were other options? What options are available to a pregnant cadet?"

Angel sighed. "Well, Jan, I think you know I would not have had an abortion. But that was one option. I could also have had the baby, given it up for adoption, and then returned with the next class of incoming yearlings." Angel looked down as she continued, "I might not have chosen that option either, but none of these choices were ever presented to me. I was told I had to resign. Period. So, that's what I did."

Jan had never even thought about what she might have chosen if she had been in Angel's shoes. To date, it wasn't something that could even be possible. "Angel, once you...once you..." she didn't want to mention it, "once you had the miscarriage, could you have come back with our class?"

"I called and asked about that. Since I had only missed about two weeks, I thought maybe it was possible. But I was told that my resignation was irreversible. I had already made a decision to quit and could not reverse that choice."

"Who did you speak to, Angel?"

Angel sighed again. "I spoke to my Buckner TAC the first time. When he told me I could not return, I decided to try someone higher up the chain of command. I called the commandant's office and spoke with LTC Cunningham. He told me the same thing: I could not return once I had resigned. I gave up after that."

"So what are you going to do now, Angel?"

"I've enrolled in a few night classes at our community college and I'm applying to Columbia. They said my chances are good that I can get a scholarship next semester."

"I'm so glad to hear that." Jan knew Angel could not afford to attend college otherwise.

They exchanged home addresses and phone numbers, hugged and promised to keep in touch. Jan felt sure Angel would keep her end of the deal. She wasn't so sure about her own end. Sometimes best intentions just weren't enough. But she would try. She would definitely try.

Kristi and Pamela were sitting on her bed when she returned Sunday night. Jan filled them in on what happened at the panel and her meeting with Angel. She told them about the mysterious Cadet Wan, whom Captain Hasuko desperately wanted to contact.

"Wait, I heard about her," Pamela said. "She was dating the comm's son, I think."

"Hasuko mentioned something about that when he tried to convince Jurgensen that they needed to hear from her," Jan said. "But the chair wasn't interested in pursuing her story."

"That's because she accused the comm's son of rape," Pamela said. "She was a cow in Fourth Regiment, I think. I heard a couple of guys in my electrical engineering class talking about it."

"What happened?" Jan asked.

"Apparently, they had a big fight and broke up. Then he came to her room later that same night and forced her to have sex. That's rape in my book. Her roommate was away at a swim meet. She reported it up her chain of command, but he said they were dating and it was consensual sex."

"Are you shitting me?" Pamela asked.

"He was given a fifty-hour slug for 'inappropriate conduct in the barracks' or something like that. She was promptly charged with an Honor violation. She knew she wouldn't win so she decided to quit instead."

"Jesus H. Christ," Jan said.

"Yeah, even He couldn't help her," Kristi added.

"Damn, I wonder if that's why Jurgensen didn't want Hasuko to pursue her testimony," Jan thought out loud.

"Hey, what's his first name?" Kristi asked.

"Who? Hasuko? Ray, I think."

"No, Jurgensen."

"Oh, um, let me look at my notes...I wrote a few things down while I was listening." Jan pulled out a small notebook that she had carried to the panel. The last thing she wrote in it was Angel's address and phone number. Before that, she had written down the names of the women and bullet points from their testimonies. Above those names, she had written down the names of each officer on the panel.

"Benjamin. LTC Benjamin Jurgensen," Jan said.

Kristi and Pamela looked at each other and rolled their eyes.

"What?" Jan asked.

"Well, that explains why Cadet Wan didn't show up for the panel," Pamela said. "Jurgensen made sure she wouldn't be there."

"How do you know that?"

"Because we heard LTC Cunningham shouting to someone on the phone when we were waiting to meet with him. His exact words were, 'I don't want her name or face anywhere near that thing, you got it...Benjamin?'"

"Kissy, he could have been talking about anything...maybe..."

"Jan, c'mon, he's the comm's assistant. I'll bet you another hundred hours of walking tours—that's exactly what he was talking about."

Jan thought for a moment. It was too much of a coincidence. Kristi was right: The commandant protected his son by making sure LTC Cunningham made sure LTC Jurgensen made sure Cadet Wan didn't show up.

That's when Jan decided she would find out Cadet Wan's version of events. *Come hell or hot water!*

Jan continued unpacking her duffel bag as Pamela and Kristi told her about their weekend. It was typical: They took a long run on Saturday to make up for all the beer they would drink Saturday night, then they slept through Sunday afternoon to recover. Most weekends weren't even that good if you counted SAMI (Saturday AM Inspection,) Parades, and for the chosen few, Walking Tours.

"Did you get lucky with Rick?" Kristi asked in her subtle way.

"Kissy! You know he barely speaks to me these days." Jan hung her dress gray in the closet and put on her USMA sweats.

"So? You don't have to talk to have sex. Or was he with the hyena again?" Pamela asked.

"The bad news is we didn't talk. The good news is he wasn't with Caroline, either." Jan put her dirty clothes into the green laundry bag in the pull-down cabinet next to the sink.

Pamela said, "Well, that's a good sign."

"She's pretty enough, I guess, but she's so freaking annoying with that laugh of hers. Not to mention she never stops talking." Jan began brushing her teeth.

"I still think he likes you, Jan," Pamela said.

With her mouth full of foaming toothpaste Jan said, "I fill fike him, foo." She spit into the sink and wiped her mouth with a towel. "But you can only lead a horse to water, you can't make them bathe."

Myrna walked in just as Jan picked up her folded Gray Girl from the end of her bed. She wrapped herself in it and slumped down on her rack.

"Jan, what the hell happened to your Gray Girl?" Myrna asked.

"What do you mean?" Jan looked down at her warm, cozy comforter, not seeing anything wrong.

"Oh, shit." Kristi walked over and straightened out the portion around Jan's legs.

Then she saw it clearly. A giant "X" over the name "WISHART" had been burned into her Gray Girl by cigarettes or cigars.

FOURTEEN

"I am extraordinarily patient, provided I get my own way in the end."
(Margaret Thatcher)

November 28, 1982
1730 hours

The trio spent Thanksgiving at the Wishart home drinking, eating and sleeping their way through most of the weekend before taking a Greyhound bus to New York City on Saturday. The plan was to stay with Drew one night in his tiny apartment before returning to Woo Poo U on Sunday.

Jan had not seen Drew since his expulsion from USMA the previous year. Technically, he resigned. Jan still felt angry every time she thought about how and why he left. He had been her best friend in Beast and the only male friend she made all last year, not counting the anonymous one.

Everyone knew gays and lesbians would never be allowed in the military, at least not openly. The Army policy was *not* "Don't ask, don't tell." It was "Don't be gay." In Drew's case, Jan felt fairly certain he had been falsely accused—that he was run out as a retaliation or a form of bullying—until she saw him again on the Saturday after Thanksgiving.

He greeted them at the bus station wearing a white button-down shirt, overly tight jeans, penny loafers without socks and a pink bow tie. He had taken off his black pea coat and black, pink and white plaid scarf, which he had draped over one arm as he hugged Jan and Kristi. Jan knew this was not standard wear for most guys. Then she thought about their conversations last year and all the times they had been drinking together. Drew never made a pass at her. Now that she thought about it, he never looked at her in "that way," the way a woman knows that a man is interested. Drew never seemed the slightest bit sexually attracted to Jan, and that's perhaps the reason why she trusted him more than anyone else last year. He had been her best friend—more like a girlfriend. Jan's light bulb finally came on in that moment.

Drew IS gay.

The four friends piled into a booth at the pizza place near his apartment. They all ordered beers and the largest, most heavily decorated pizza on the menu. The women filled him in on the latest news from their home on the Hudson. Jan told about her "almost" encounter with Rick Davidson in the dayroom and how he seemed to have moved on to the hyena from Team Handball. She acted as though she no longer wanted anything to do with Rick, which of course wasn't true. They also informed him about Violet's firstie boyfriend, who seemed to be a bit of a bully. They described Violet's ability to lose and gain weight every couple months, a feat that totally perplexed them. They filled him in on the weigh-ins, the diet tables and the body fat testing. Drew had known all about these things from last year but he was surprised to hear they were still a part of their lives in yearling year. Jan shared the incident with Major Stanley and how Rick promised to intervene if it happened again. She talked about her new nemesis in G-1, John Heggenbach, who seemed to be the resident hard-ass, and about her new roommate, Myrna, a know-it-all lesbian.

All of the pizza and most of their third round of beers were gone when they finally exhausted the current events at West Point. "Wait! We forgot to mention the most significant stuff," Kristi announced excitedly. "First, Angel Trane quit just before the start of the academic year. And second, someone's been vandalizing my things." Kristi proceeded to explain the dead snake, pissed shoes and slashed textbooks.

Jan couldn't believe they had overlooked mentioning those things before. They *were* the most significant events. She wondered if they subconsciously wanted to avoid talking about it. She proceeded to inform Drew about everything she learned from Captain Hasuko's panel and specifically, why Angel had resigned.

"What was her plan for the baby? Was she going to keep it?" Drew asked.

Jan said, "I think she was planning to raise it or give it up for adoption. She wouldn't have had an abortion, of course, not with her religious beliefs."

"If she had chosen adoption she could have returned to West Point, right?"

"Apparently that was an option. Although she wasn't told about it, she was told she had to resign," Jan said.

"Could she have returned after her miscarriage? I mean, if that's what she wanted?" he asked.

"She tried and was told she could not come back since she had already resigned," Jan said. "However, Major Behar has given me a little more information."

Kristi leaned forward. "What did the Arab tell you?"

"Kristi!" Although Major Behar was Arab, Jan didn't like that Kristi used the term in a derogatory way.

Pamela and Drew now leaned over the table so that the four of them looked like they were whispering together over the pizza crumbs.

"Well, Major Behar and a small group of professors are looking into the high numbers of resignations and expulsions of female cadets. She told me that only a few involved pregnancy, yet none of the women were told of other options, including returning after their pregnancy, once they gave up legal responsibility for the child."

"So you're saying they were told their *only* choice was to resign?" Pamela asked.

"Yes, exactly. Two of those women, Angel included, inquired about returning to the Corps after their pregnancies were over. Both were told it was not possible."

"But they actually would have been allowed to go back?" Drew asked.

"Yes, if they did not have legal custody of a child, then they could return within a certain window of time. I think they had one year to make the decision," Jan said, realizing Angel could technically come back with the next crop of yearlings.

"What else did Behar tell you?" Pamela asked.

"She said that some of the women resigned for post-traumatic stress, usually after reporting an incident of rape or other serious harassment. They, too, were never informed of their options for counseling, medical leave or legal action which might have affected their decision. Major Behar said in almost every case, women who complained of being abused or harassed were pressured to resign."

"How many were kicked out?" Drew asked.

"She said the majority were quasi-voluntary resignations. However, a small number left for academic failure and an even smaller number for disciplinary reasons. She also said one woman resigned after being charged with an Honor violation, which never went to trial." Jan thought that wasn't such a bad choice.

"But who would even want to come back after those things—getting pregnant or being abused—who would want to face the place again?" Pamela asked.

"That's not the point, Pamela. The point is, *none of these women even knew they had a choice*," Kristi said.

"What's even more troubling," Jan added, "is that 'problem women,'" Jan used her fingers as quotation marks, "are thrown out before they even know what hit them."

The four friends sat silently for a while, contemplating what seemed to be institutional hazing of traumatized women.

"Well, I'm afraid the Academy still has a few 'problem women' on its hands," Kristi said, copying the quotation mark gesture Jan had just used.

They all laughed for a few moments before getting back down to business. After another hour and one more round of beers, they were ready to leave.

"Great. We have a plan then," Drew stated.

"I guess so. It's just that I was hoping things could be normal for us this year," Jan sighed.

"Jan, what's 'normal' about West Point?" Kristi asked, using her finger quotes again.

"I know, I know. I just wanted a little peace and quiet for one year."

"You'll have plenty of that when you die," Kristi said, smirking.

FIFTEEN

"Success is not final, failure is not fatal: it is the courage to continue that counts."
(Winston Churchill)

December 4, 1982
1900 hours

The annual war between the service academies began the first weekend in December. Buses transported the entire Corps of Cadets to Veterans Memorial Stadium in Philadelphia to cheer on the Army team in its epic battle against the evil Naval Academy. But, alas, it was to no avail. The bad guys won again.

Terribly disappointed plebes would be required to hug the walls for a few more months. For Jan and most of her friends, the outcome of the game was of little significance. What mattered most was being away from the gray walls and gray halls of West Point and having a whole weekend, other than the short interlude of the game itself, to party.

They got right down to business as soon as they hit the hotels and changed into their civvies. Jan had bought a new outfit at the C-Store (Cadet Store)—blue corduroy pants and a beige sweater—specifically for this gala event. Never having a need for civilian attire most of the year, the Army/Navy weekend was her excuse to buy something special. High fashion, it was not. It wasn't even medium fashion, but at least it was new.

Jan was supposed to share a room with the other G-1 yearling women, but since Lisa would spend all her time with the softball team, and Esther would spend all her time with her yearling boyfriend, and Leslie would spend all her time in the room, Jan opted for Plan B. She moved into the H-1 women's room with Pamela, Kristi and Violet. They didn't bother asking Violet's permission since she would spend all her time with Joey Lishiski.

After eating a hurried dinner, the trio returned to their room to brush their teeth. The sound of regurgitation greeted them when they entered the room. Kristi put her forefinger to her pursed lips as they quietly slipped by the closed bathroom door. Jan and Pamela sat on one queen bed, while Kristi stood near the television dresser. They stared at each other in wide-eyed in silence.

For Jan and Kristi, hearing Violet throwing up behind a locked bathroom door brought back vivid and frightening memories. The exact thing happened last year over the Army/Navy weekend, when they discovered their company mate, Debra Plowden, throwing up in the bathroom. Debra had been raped.

Jan pointed to her watch and mouthed, "It's too early for that."

Kristi knew exactly what she meant. It was too early for anyone to be drunk and too early for any other nefarious activity. Surely it couldn't be a repeat of last year.

They heard the toilet flush, then running water, teeth brushing and the squeak of the sink faucet. The door opened and Violet emerged.

"Oh, hey, I didn't hear you guys come in." She sounded almost cheery.

"We just came back to brush our teeth before heading out again," Pamela said.

"Are you okay, Violet?" Jan asked.

"Yeah, I'm fine," she replied.

"We heard you throwing up," Kristi stated.

"Way to beat around the bushel, Kissy." Jan shot a glance at her former roommate.

Kristi shot a look right back. "So are you sick, Violet?"

"No, I'm fine. Must've eaten something that didn't agree with me, that's all."

The trio looked at each other skeptically.

"What? You don't believe me?" Violet asked defensively.

Pamela said, "We've smelled throw-up a few times after you've been in the latrine. Is this something you do regularly?"

"No," she said with a steely tone. "I guess I have a sensitive stomach."

Weak stomachs were not a common problem among female cadets. But maybe Violet did have something that caused her to get sick more often than others. This wasn't their area of expertise. Perhaps Violet had some kind of condition. It was none of their business, anyway.

"Well, you should go on sick call if it doesn't get better," Pamela said.

"Yeah, maybe they can give you something for it—nausea medicine or something," Kristi added.

"I might just do that," Violet answered. "Gotta run now, meeting Joey in five." She hurried out the door.

"There's something wrong with her," Jan said. "She loses and gains weight every other month. Noticeable weight."

"And she always has bruises that she blames on clumsiness," Pamela added.

"Well, we all know what that's about," Kristi said. "Joey gets his kicks out of, well, kicking Violet."

"Have you two tried to talk to her about that?" Jan asked.

"Yes, we have. She ignores us or changes the subject," Pamela said. "She won't admit what he's doing to her."

"Should we tell someone?" Jan wondered out loud. "Can we talk to your TAC?"

"Yeah, we could tell him what we know about Violet. But honestly, if she's stupid enough to put up with Joey's bullshit, I don't really feel sorry for her," Kristi said.

"I'm not sure it's our place to say anything, anyway," Pamela added. "If she's not willing to admit anything, we could just get her in more trouble."

"I suppose you're right," Jan said. "It just seems so shitty. I sure as hell would never let anyone get away with that crap."

"Violet's not like us, Jan," Kristi said, "she has a weak stomach, remember?"

Jan chuckled. "Yeah, I guess we're cut from very different fabric."

Pamela and Kristi started giggling.

"What?" Jan didn't see what was so funny.

"Nothing, Jan. You just march to your own trumpeter." Pamela stood up. "Now, let's go find a party."

They found one in room 737. With the doors open to the adjoining rooms, the space could hold at least thirty cadets. Jan, Pamela and Kristi mingled with yearlings, cows and a few firsties from G, H and I companies. The bathtub in the center room had been filled with bottles of beer, wine and hard liquor, all submerged in ice. Jan planned to spend the night drinking and, if possible, flirting.

Rick Davidson stood by the window in the middle room. He looked away as soon as Jan smiled at him. *Well, that was short-lived.*

She moved to the far left room where John Heggenbach and two other G-1 firsties stood drinking beer and laughing. Esther Gonsalez leaned against her boyfriend, Adam Nutter.

If they ever get married, she should keep her own last name.

"Hey, Esther." Jan moved toward her company mate.

"Jan, how's it going?"

"Good, thanks." She looked around. "Lisa and Leslie coming?"

"No, Lisa is with her team. And you know Leslie, Jan. She doesn't do this kind of thing."

"Yeah, I just thought maybe she'd make an exception. You know, Army/Navy and all." They both chuckled.

Jan didn't know anything about Esther Gonsalez, but since she was one of only three yearling women in G-1, they would eventually be roommates, probably several times. Maybe, Jan hoped, they could also be friends. *Too bad her boyfriend is always in the picture.*

Jan continued to socialize with Esther, Adam and the other G-1 firsties. She kept her back to John Heggenbach, however, not wanting to talk to him. The drinking continued and more cadets showed up until the room filled way beyond the fire code capacity.

Jan's and John's backs became mushed together, although she didn't realize it until he reached his right hand around and squeezed the front of her thigh. She grabbed his hand and returned it to its rightful place. When he reached his hand around again, she let it stay there. Then she dropped her hand to his, rubbing it softly.

Yes, I'm willing.

The room was too crowded for anyone to see the shenanigans and for anything more to happen there. They would have to escape.

He turned his head to whisper in her left ear. "Fourth floor stairwell, west side of the building, fifteen minutes. Can you do that?"

She paused long enough to appear hesitant. She turned her head to her left and whispered, "Which way is west?"

She heard him chuckle. "Go left out of the door."

"Okay," she said.

"You sure?"

She thought it gentlemanly of him to ask. "Yes."

"See you, then." She felt his presence vacate from behind her. She turned her head to see him exit the door and turn left.

Oh shit. What am I doing? John Heggenbach? Jan, you've had way too much to drink.

She knew she would not have agreed to meet him if she had been sober. Certainly, she never expected *him* to be her "first." But she was growing old waiting to lose her virginity. And she wanted to know what all the hullabaloo was about. *Let's just do this thing.*

She found Pamela back in the middle room talking with Rick and a few other classmates. Jan whispered in her ear, "I'm going out for a bit. I'll either meet you guys back here or in our room."

Pamela arched an eyebrow at her and whispered, "Who?"

Jan shrugged her shoulders. "Firstie, in my company. Tell you all about it later."

"Name?"

"Heggenbach," Jan whispered, "don't mention to ANYONE."

"Okay, be safe." Pamela winked. "You know what I mean, right?"

"Yes, yes. All taken care of." Jan smiled thinking how close they had become in such a short time. No one could take Kristi's place, but Pamela was quickly becoming a fixture in Jan's heart.

She pushed the door open and hesitated. An industrial railing snaked up and down the stairs and a fire extinguisher was strapped to the opposite wall. It was completely lit, brighter than the hallway.

This won't do.

John pulled the door all the way open from behind it. "Are you just gonna stand there?"

She stepped into the stairwell; he pushed the door closed and pulled her toward him. Their lips met in a long, fiery kiss, followed by several more.

She put her hands on his chest and pushed back for a moment. "Don't you think this is a bit...bright?"

"It's not ideal," he agreed, "shall we try to find somewhere else?"

"I'd prefer it, if you don't mind."

He leaned against the iron railing. "Not at all. There's just not a lot of options in a hotel that's filled with a few hundred cadets. And I can guarantee you that plenty of them are trying to find the same kind of spot we are."

Jan thought out loud. "They should just reserve a few extra rooms for this thing."

He started laughing. "Yeah, they could call them 'comfort rooms.'"

"Well," she felt her face turn red, "they have to know this kind of thing will happen."

"You're funny, Jan, you know that?"

He was drunk. She knew because that wasn't the kind of thing John Heggenbach would say. This wasn't the kind of thing John Heggenbach would normally do, either.

"Let's just go to my room," she said. "My roommates won't be back for hours, and even if they do come back, they won't turn us in."

"You sure?" This was the second time he asked that in the same night.

"Yes, I'll go first, then you follow in about ten minutes. Room 419."

He hungrily kissed her again and for a moment she wasn't sure they would make it out of the stairwell. She pulled away, turned around and ran down the stairs, entering the hallway again at the fourth floor.

She lost her virginity to John Heggenbech that night. Only Jan would not say she lost it, so much, as she gave it up. Albeit, she had been drinking a lot. Still, she willingly allowed the events to unfold. She wanted to get it out of the way. It had been hanging over her like a big, dark shadow—always something everyone else knew about, but not her.

Even Angel has done it.

Now she was in the club. And then she wondered what all the fuss was about.

She could understand why guys loved it so much. Something seemed to happen to John. He shuddered before collapsing on top of her. Other than a bit of pressure at first, she hadn't felt anything spectacular.

Was that it? Are we done?

John seemed embarrassed. He got up without saying anything, put his pants back on, then kissed her once more before leaving the room. Jan stayed lying in the bed for several minutes.

Well, that was...interesting.

She talked herself into going back upstairs to the party in room 737, which took a bit of work because she was now petrified of seeing John Heggenbach. Yet she knew she had to do it. In fact, she had to beat him there. She had to show that this meant nothing—that Jan Wishart could be just like a guy. She could have sex and move on. She was not a wimpy girl who needed anyone to "love" her. She would go back into that room and hold her head high, by God.

She didn't beat him to the room, however. She entered the party just after John returned and shortly after they both had been missing for close to an hour. Everyone seemed to turn and look at her when she passed through the open doorway. Jan's eyes met Rick's and she felt her neck go red for the second time that night. She knew that he knew.

"That didn't take long." Pamela seemed to come to Jan's rescue.

"Yeah, just ran back to the room for a while," Jan said, hoping some would think she had to make a phone call or something. It wasn't a lie, of course.

"Did you find what you were looking for?" Pamela asked loudly enough for others to hear.

"Yes, yes. It was...right...where...I left it."

"It was?" Pamela looked concerned.

"Yes, well, not exactly." Jan widened her eyes.

"Oh, okay. Good."

"Yes, it's all good."

Maybe it was the disappointment with sex, maybe it was the disappointment in Rick's eyes, or maybe it was the disappointment she felt in herself, but she proceeded to get even more drunk. She remembered having four beers "before John," and then she had at least three more "after John," along with several shots of whiskey. That didn't include the couple of glasses of wine thrown in for good measure.

By 0400, the room had mostly emptied out. Kristi, Pamela and a handful of diehards still loitered around. Rick and John were still there too. Jan wondered if they were having a contest to see who would leave first. She had been sitting on one of the beds and wanted to flop over and fall asleep right there. Which she probably could have done, since no one seemed to actually have laid claim to the room.

Instead, she stood up, signaled to Kristi and Pamela that she wanted to leave and headed toward the door. Her body had another plan. She fell face down on the carpet, which didn't hurt nearly as much as it should have.

Two people lifted her up, one on each side. "Thanks, guys," she said, thinking they were Pamela and Kristi.

"No problem," John Heggenbach said on her right.

"We'll help you back to your room," she heard Rick say from her left.

She started laughing. "This is sooooo...perrfet."

"What's so funny?" Rick asked.

It took a while for her to stop laughing enough to say, "This."

"This, what?" John asked.

"You two. And me," she said between hysterics.

The two men looked at each other. John didn't have a clue, but Rick had some idea of what she found so funny. He didn't seem to think it was funny at all.

Jan woke up with the mother of all headaches. It felt like someone had shoved an ice pick between her eyes. She shuffled to the bathroom, turned on the tap and stuck her head, mouth up, under the tepid water. After guzzling about a gallon she walked slowly back to the bed she was sharing with Pamela. Kristi had the other bed to herself, since Violet never returned to the room.

As soon as she sank under the sheets Pamela whispered, "So tell me what happened last night when you left."

"Geez," Jan sighed, "it was weird." She rolled onto her back and tried to focus on the ceiling. It hurt too much to keep her eyes open so she closed them. "I can't believe...John Heggenbach. My first time." She took a long, deep breath. "That was probably not my best decision."

"Was that your first time?" Pamela asked.

"Yeah. Stupid, huh?"

"No, I wasn't thinking that. I'm just surprised, that's all."

"I know. I'm a late bloomer."

"Not as late as me, though."

Jan rolled onto her side facing Pamela. "You're a virgin, too? I mean, still?" She thought she had been the only one left—of her friends, anyway.

"Yeah," Pamela said, rolling over onto her back. "Guess I'm the last one now."

"Well, as far as I can tell, you're not missing much," Jan said. "Of course, maybe it feels better when you're with someone you care about or love. I wouldn't know about that yet."

"I hear it's supposed to feel great," Pamela said.

"So they say..."

"You two are killing me!" On the other bed, Kristi rolled onto her side so she faced them. "Haven't you ever heard of masturbation?" When Jan and Pamela didn't answer, she added, "Oh my God! You have no idea, do you?"

"We've heard of it, Kissy, of course," Jan knew guys did it. She had no idea women could too.

"But...?" Kristi asked. Jan and Pamela remained silent. "But—you've never done it, right?"

"Right," they both answered.

"Well, you're on your own this time. I sure as hell can't teach you *everything*."

Jan turned on the shower. She waited on the toilet seat until the room completely fogged. Then she stripped off her t-shirt and underwear, stepped into the bathtub and let the scalding water pound her head. She figured it couldn't possibly hurt more on the outside than it did on the inside.

Do you feel better now? The question popped into her head from God knows where. She hadn't been thinking it, she certainly hadn't asked it. It just came to the surface, like an old letter that was lost in the mail and then delivered years later to its intended recipient.

"What?" She whispered out loud to herself—or to whoever asked the other question.

But no reply came. Instead, the question reverberated in her aching head. *Do you feel better now? Do you feel better? Do you feel? Do you?*

Jan answered in hot tears that streamed down her face, becoming lost in the scorching water from the showerhead.

SIXTEEN

"History will show that no man rose to military greatness who could not convince his troops that he put them first."
(General Maxwell Taylor, USMA Class of 1922)

December 7, 1982
1330 hours

Major Stanley behaved properly ever since that first incident at the boards in September. It had been so long since then that Jan began wondering if she had imagined the situation worse than it really was. That might have been why she didn't realize he was up to no good again, until he was up to no good again.

"Take boards," Major Stanley ordered. Each cadet stood and faced a section of the chalkboard, while the physics professor read aloud a problem they were to work on alone, he stated. That meant no one would look around at anyone else's work. Everyone would keep their eyes directly on their own section of the chalkboard.

Jan began contemplating the equation when she felt the professor standing directly behind her, pressing against her again. She had both arms at her sides with a piece of chalk in her right hand. She sensed his right arm coming around her body, reaching for her breast. This time she was ready, and before his hand found its target, she jerked around to her left in one swift motion.

"Sir, did you say acceleration was 3.2 meters per second?"

She knocked him off balance, causing him to fall backwards onto a cadet's desk and then completely over onto the floor, sending books and papers flying.

"Oh, my goodness, sir, I didn't realize you were standing so close behind me," Jan said, putting her hands over her mouth. She said a silent thank you for those plebe year self-defense classes. They finally came in handy.

The rest of the class, all male cadets, turned around and watched as Major Stanley began righting himself. Rick looked at Jan with a raised eyebrow. She responded with a slight nod and smile. Then he furrowed his brow.

Major Stanley stood up. "Miss Wishart, please be more careful in the future."

"Sir, perhaps *you* should be more careful," Rick said seriously while the class erupted in laughter.

"Everyone back to work!" Major Stanley shouted.

Jan looked at Rick and smiled. He winked back.

They left Mahan Hall together and talked for the first time since the Team Handball trip to Montreal.

"Thanks for speaking up back there," she said.

"I wanted that asshole to know that I'm on to him. Hopefully he won't bother you again."

"It had been so long since his last attempt that I figured he had reformed. Guess not, huh?"

"No, they never reform," Rick said. "I'm sorry I couldn't do more to help, I didn't notice...again." He shook his head.

"It's not your fault."

"I know it's not, but I feel like I should be able to help more—and to keep shit like that from happening."

"You did help. You said something. He got the message. And you're talking to me now. That's huge."

"Jan, I'm sorry about Montreal. I got drunk..."

"Rick, you don't need to explain that. But I would like to know why you started ignoring me. You seemed angry at me and I have no idea what I did."

"Myrna told me to leave you alone. She said you needed space and that I was keeping you from making new friends."

"What?" Jan practically shouted. "I never said anything even remotely like that!"

"Well, she made it seem like you didn't want to speak to me anymore. So I tried to make it easy for you."

"That's bullshit. I'm going to have a 'Come to Jesus' with her."

"So, it's not true?"

"No, Rick. I don't know why she told you that."

"Damn. Montreal would never have happened if I thought you were available."

"Okay, let's not bring that up again. It's history. Let's just leave it there. Besides, if you apologize, then I have to apologize too—and you know that's not my strong suit."

"For Army/Navy weekend?"

"Well, yeah, since you put it like that."

"That really killed me."

"Thanks, Rick. I felt guilty enough without hearing that."

"I'm just letting you know how much it hurt me. But it was only fair after what I did to you in Montreal."

"Wait a minute, Rick. We were never a couple, we didn't..."

"But we should be," he interrupted.

They stopped walking. They stood facing each other in the middle of Thayer Road, both in black parkas with black and gold striped beanies on their heads and an armload of books. A light dusting of snow had blanketed the street and gray buildings while soft powder continued to dance its way to the ground. The whole scene reminded Jan of a Currier and Ives lithograph.

Rick stepped closer to Jan, their faces only inches apart. From a distance, anyone might think he was a firstie scolding a beanhead. Anywhere else, it would be perfectly acceptable if they kissed right there, out in the open, in front of God and everyone. But at West Point, PDA (Public Display of Affection) was forbidden. Hand holding, hugging and kissing were never seen at the United States Military Academy.

Despite the rules, Jan didn't back away when Rick leaned in and planted a swift, but determined, kiss on her lips.

"Took you long enough," Jan said.

"You didn't exactly make it easy for me, Jan."

"No, that's what Caroline does." She smirked.

"Now, that's not fair." He smiled back.

They walked together toward New South by heading up the ramp from Thayer Road. About halfway up, they witnessed what seemed like a firstie reprimanding a beanhead.

"No way, uh-uh, Vy. We can't change our plans now."

Jan and Rick stopped walking, watching in amazement. It wasn't a firstie and a plebe interaction. It was Joey Lishiski seemingly chastising Violet Carpetta.

"Why not? It's only a couple days," Violet said in a quiet voice.

"Because we've already bought the tickets and reserved the rooms."

"But..." she trailed off, noticing Jan and Rick standing down the ramp from them.

Apparently Joey hadn't noticed them. "I'm done talking, Violet, no use gibbering on about it."

Violet nodded at Joey, letting him know they were being watched. Joey turned his head, and upon seeing Jan and Rick, he quickly looked down at his shoes. Violet turned to Jan. "Hey, Jan, how's it going?"

Why does she let him talk to her like that? She shook out of her trance and resumed walking up the ramp with Rick. "Hey, Violet, what's up?"

"Not much. Hey, Rick, how are you?" Violet forced a smile.

"I'm good, Violet, thanks, and you?"

"Fine, thanks."

Rick and Jan began passing Violet and Joey on their right. But Jan couldn't stand the thought of leaving Violet there without *saying something*—without *doing something*. Yet she didn't know what to say or do.

Rick did it for her. "Joey, you really ought to get that looked at."

"What looked at?" Joey asked sternly.

"Your fucking attitude. It sucks, man."

Jan had forgotten how much influence Rick had, even with upperclassmen. Because he had been prior service, because he earned a combat patch, because he was older than most of the firsties, he commanded respect.

Joey exploded. "Hey man, you got nothing to do with this, so I'd keep my trap shut if I were you."

Rick didn't even skip a beat. "Well, thankfully you're not me."

Joey knew he had been put in his place and he didn't even try to fight back.

"Good job, Rick," Jan whispered as they walked passed the quarrelling lovers. "That's twice in one day you've managed to come up with something brilliant."

"Yeah, well, 'brilliant' is my middle name."

"Oh God, I've opened Pandora's bag now..."

Rick's laughter seemed to reverberate off the stone buildings and echo all the way down the Hudson River.

"Why the hell did you tell Rick to leave me alone?" Jan confronted Myrna as soon as she entered her room.

"What?"

"You heard me, Myrna. You told Rick to stay away from me. Why?"

"I didn't tell him to stay away from you, I told him it would be better for you to make new friends, that's all."

"What the hell is that supposed to mean?" Jan fumed.

"It means that you came to G-1 with a certain reputation and hanging out with the same guys from your old company doesn't help you to move beyond that. I was just trying to help, Jan."

"First of all, that's bullshit. Rick doesn't hurt my reputation at all. Secondly, if you really felt that way, you would have told Kristi to stop hanging out with me, not Rick." Jan slammed her books down on her desk. "Thirdly, it's none of your goddamn business who I choose to hang out with."

"You are getting way too hot under the collar about this, Jan. I'm not going to even try to explain anymore, since you are so damn upset by it."

"What the hell? You're not my mother, Myrna."

"No shit, Sherlock. But you still could use a little help after the mess you got into last year. I was just trying to make things a little easier for you this year."

"No you're not, you just didn't want me dating Rick. Are you jealous, Myrna?" As soon as Jan said it, she knew she had stepped over the line.

In a flash, Myrna jumped out of her chair and was in Jan's face, like a firstie on a plebe. "You better watch your goddamn tongue, Jan, or I'll cut the fucking thing out. You better NEVER say anything like that to me again." She grabbed Jan's shirt collar. "Or I'll beat the living shit out of you. Got me?"

Even though Jan was about a foot taller than Myrna, the little sparkplug was more than capable of taking her down. Also, Myrna had the power, as a cow, to make Jan's life miserable.

She relented. "Okay, Myrna, sorry for my choice of words." Myrna let go of Jan's shirt and stepped back. "I just don't understand why you said anything to Rick, who I happen to like very much."

"You can do better than him, that's why!"

She is jealous. "Well, I prefer to make my own choices about that kind of thing, and I would appreciate it if you wouldn't say things to people without my permission."

"I'll say whatever the hell I want," Myrna said, going back to her chair.

Jan decided it was best to let Myrna have the last word.

SEVENTEEN

"The art of war is simple enough. Find out where your enemy is. Get at him as soon as you can. Strike at him as hard as you can, and keep moving on."
(General Ulysses S. Grant, USMA Class of 1843)

December 10, 1982
0700 hours

The entire Corps of Cadets became eerily quiet as everyone began preparing for the last hurdle before Christmas break. Once Term End Exams began, everyone's sleeping time would decrease by half. On the Friday morning before exam week, however, after the plebes delivered *The New York Times* to every cadet room, Jan realized she would lose even more sleep. In the *Issues* section was the following article:

What's Happening to Women at West Point?
(Part 1)
By Steve Calibrio, staff writer

Many of us cheered for the brave few women who entered the gates of West Point for the first time in the summer of 1976. We cheered again when that first class with women graduated in

May 1980. Since then, we have been celebrating the accomplishments, milestones and surprising adaptability of the United States Military Academy as it transitioned from an all-male institution to one that includes women. We felt proud of the United States Military Academy, the Army, and our country for its ability to embrace this sea change with seemingly only the slightest of hiccups.

Now, six years on, we are discovering something is wrong with the picture. We've been wearing rose-colored glasses, or worse, we've been duped. We've been led to believe that things are fine—when things are certainly NOT fine—for many women at West Point.

Pardon me for using a saying I learned in basic training: "We need to get our heads out of our asses" and find out what's really going on. Something is happening. Something dark and menacing is causing an unusually high number of women to resign or to be expelled.

When I tried to get the statistics from the Academy's admissions office, I was directed to the Office of the Commandant of Cadets. From there, I was routed to the Office of the Dean where I was told I would need to call the admissions office for any information on female cadets. I tried again at admissions where I was directed, yet again, to the commandant's office. Suffice it to say that it appears West Point either does not keep records or they do not want this information to be made public.

Unfortunately for them, my reliable source is in touch with a few women who are walking tall at West Point. Here's what has been provided to me via these few, good women:

1. *Almost 25% (44) of female plebes (freshman) have resigned this year alone.*
2. *The dropout/expulsion rate for women in all classes is 25% higher than the rate for men in all classes.*
3. *Women are resigning at a higher rate than men. The ratio of resignations to expulsions for women is 8:2. The same ratio for men is 5:5.*

4. Of the 35 women we located, 28 gave a specific reason for leaving West Point. Of those, 24 women left due to some form of sexual harassment and/or abuse. Fifteen of those women admitted to being sexually assaulted.

5. Each class starts with approximately 12% to 15% of women cadets. The class of 1985, the largest in the history of West Point, began with approximately 1500 cadets. Of those, 213 were women. Only 160 women reported for the beginning of yearling (sophomore) year. At this rate, the class of 1985 will graduate less than 100 women—over 50% attrition.

If these numbers are even close to the truth, then it's even more disturbing that this information could not be obtained through official channels. If the numbers are inaccurate, which I doubt, we still have to wonder why West Point seems to be keeping it secret. What are they hiding?

Fortunately, a small network of concerned officers at West Point gathered this information and shared it with a few female cadets, who released it to my colleague. They did so at great personal risk. When this article appears, there may be repercussions for all female cadets.

Again, when I called the Office of Admissions to confirm this information, I was ignored, rebuffed and put on hold indefinitely. I can only assume the Academy's silence on this matter means the Gals in Gray have succeeded in securing accurate information.

The bigger questions still need to be addressed:

1) What, if anything, is being done to address the concerns, violations, abuse, and/or prejudice against women at West Point?

2) Does the Academy provide any training and/or education about sexual harassment and sexual violence?

3) Are female cadets fully informed of their rights?

4) Are there clear avenues for reporting abuses? Are women heard and believed when they come forward with a complaint?

5) What actions are taken once a female cadet reports a violation? Is she supported and encouraged or is she ostracized?

The answers to these questions seem to be as elusive as the "Ghost in the Lost Fifties," from cadet folklore. I know there are many like me who long to cheer on the brave old Army team once again. It's just hard to do when you know that some teammates are being sidelined and eliminated from the roster, apparently for no good reason. In fact, they seem to be disappearing for bad reasons—very bad reasons.

No one can cheer for that.

Jan slammed the paper down on the sink counter.

"Dammit!"

"What is it?" Myrna asked, sitting on the side of her bed.

"Read this." Jan handed the paper to her roommate and stood, trance-like, in the middle of the room while Myrna read the article.

"This doesn't involve you, does it?" Myrna asked. When Jan still didn't move, she said, "Oh, shit."

"What am I going to do, Myrna?"

Myrna stood up, placing the paper on her desk and letting out a sigh. "You're going to act normally. You're going to pretend you had nothing to do with it."

"But what if I'm asked? What if someone comes right out and asks, 'did you have anything to do with this article?'"

"Then you have to say 'yes.' Or you could say you would rather not answer that question. Or you could just NOT answer the question. Whatever you do, they will know you DID have something to do with the article."

Myrna was right. Jan could not lie if asked directly. And by simply not answering the question directly, everyone would know she was one of the "Gals in Gray." Once one person knew the truth, the entire Corps of Cadets would know the truth.

"Shit, shit, shit!" Jan stomped to her closet and pulled out her gray overcoat. "I'm as good as dead. Right, Myrna?" Jan's eyes began to glisten.

"Yeah, Jan. I'm sorry. This might just put the final nail in your coffin."

With her gray scarf pulled up to her nose, under gray overcoat and under gray hat, Jan rushed outside to morning formation, hoping no one would stop her. She fell into the squad line at the last moment. Her squad leader looked down the line, frowning, before reporting, "All present."

Heggenbach, in the front of the platoon saluted to the platoon leader saying, "All present or accounted for."

The platoon leader shouted the same thing to the company commander, who shouted the same thing to the battalion commander. Everyone stood at attention while the flags were presented. Then they all saluted. After that, the commanders released the companies to their first sergeants, who proceeded to read each company's announcements.

"Company-wide weigh-in tonight at 1900 hours," was the only one Jan heard.

Finally, platoon leaders handed the reins over to their sergeants, who read the unit's announcements. Jan heard Heggenbach shout, "Second platoon will meet by the men's latrines for the weigh-in. First squad at 1900 hours, second squad at 1915 hours, third squad at 1930 hours and fourth squad at 1945 hours."

He continued reading announcements that flew over Jan's head until the last one: "Cadet Wishart, report to the company commander's room immediately following this formation."

Oh, Jesus.

"Dismissed," Heggenbach shouted.

Jan pinged over to him before he could escape. "John, I have a first period class. Can I report to the commander during my free period?"

"When is that?" He seemed to bark the question.

"Just before lunch, 1100 hours."

"Okay, I'll tell him. I'm free then too, so I'll come get you."

I don't need a freaking escort! "Okay, thanks," she said before heading to her room to gather her Arabic books.

She pinged like a plebe to the classroom on the top floor of Washington Hall. She beat everyone else there, which was her intention.

Come on, Behar, don't be late today.

Major Behar was one of the few professors who usually arrived before her students. By sitting at her desk prior to the cadets' arrival, the class never had to jump to attention when she walked into the room. Jan always got the feeling Major Behar found that tradition a bit...paternalistic.

Or imperialistic.

Jan paced the room in circles, stooping only to look out the large windows facing the Plain. She looked down on the snow-covered statue of George Washington on his horse. The right front hoof of his steed was lifted, indicating he was once wounded in battle. Two lifted hooves on a statue meant the rider died in battle. The bronze national father kept his back to the stone building while facing the Hudson River, pointing toward the mountains and the water, almost as if saying: "Look out beyond this present trouble—see what is farther out."

"Miss Wishart, you're early today." Major Behar entered the room and walked to her desk.

Jan turned from her reverie. "Oh, thank God you came early, ma'am. Did you see the article in *The New York Times* this morning?"

"Yes, I saw it." The professor began unloading her army-issued bag of books, folders and papers.

"What should I say, ma'am, when I'm asked about it?"

"You have to tell the truth, of course."

"Yes, I know. But can I say anything or not say anything that might make it...better? And how can I keep your name out of it?"

"Well, Miss Wishart. We knew this kind of thing might happen once we began our task. We will have to brave it as best we can. I've been through worse and you have, too."

"Major Behar, I never meant for you to get in trouble. Hell, I never meant to get myself in any more trouble. I had no idea the article was going to spell out that the information came from 'Gals in Gray.'"

"That was the risk we both took. Do your best to say as little as possible. But also be ready for what's coming. It could get very dicey from here on out. Just try to remember that you did the right thing." Major Behar stopped speaking as another cadet entered the room. Then she whispered to Jan, "Remember, you are fighting for justice."

EIGHTEEN

"Upon the conduct of each depends the fate of all."
(Alexander the Great)

December 10, 1982
1100 hours

She felt everyone giving her the evil eye during her walk between classes and on the way back to the barracks. She held her head up, staring straight ahead, knowing she had to at least pretend to be immune to their judgment. Heggenbach was waiting for her when she returned to her room.

"Let's go," he barked.

"Okay, lemme just put my books down," she said, purposely sauntering to her desk. She wanted her body language to communicate confidence. She reached into her desk drawer, pulling out a tin of mints. "Want one?" she asked holding the container toward him.

"No, thanks."

She popped two mints in her mouth and placed the tin back in her desk. "Okay, I'm ready."

Cadet Philip Strangelowe, the CO, told Jan to take a seat. He was sitting at his desk chair. His roommate, the XO, was sitting in the other desk chair. That left the beds. Jan sat on Philip's. Heggenbach stood with his back to the closed door.

"I suppose you've read the article this morning," the CO said.

"Yes," she replied.

"And everyone thinks you and Cadet McCarron are the ones who provided the information to the newspaper."

"Everyone?"

"Everyone I have heard from. If not everyone, then almost everyone."

Jan began chewing her top lip.

Philip continued, "So are you involved?"

"Yes." She figured it was futile to deny it.

"What information did you provide, exactly?"

"All of it," she answered truthfully. *All hell is going to rain down on me now.*

"Where'd you get the information?" the CO asked.

She hesitated. He asked the question again.

"I'm not going to tell you. I'm not going to tell anyone. So you may as well save your breath, I won't answer that question."

Philip Strangelowe looked at his XO, Cadet Guy Hernandez, then back at Jan. "John," he looked toward Heggenbach by the door, "what do you think about that?"

This time Heggenbach hesitated. "We already know what we need to know. It doesn't concern us where or how she got the information."

Guy chimed in, "I agree."

Philip stood up and walked over to Jan. He stopped directly in front of her. She didn't like him looking down on her, so she began to stand. He placed his hands on her shoulders. "Stay seated," he said.

Then he placed one hand on the top of her head while keeping the other on her left shoulder. "Dear God..."

What the hell?

"Please put your protection around Jan. Watch over her and keep her safe. Let no hurt, harm or danger come to her."

Christ! Is he praying? Jan glanced up and saw his eyes were closed.

"I witness before you here and now, dear Lord, that along with my brothers in this room, we will do everything we can to protect Jan from danger. Be with us in this endeavor."

Jan turned her head and saw Guy's eyes were closed. She looked toward the door and even John's eyes were closed. *Jaysus.*

"We ask this in your great name, our Savior, Jesus Christ. Amen." The other two men echoed the last word.

Then she heard herself say it.

"Amen."

Thank you, Lord!

Kristi and Pamela walked into Jan's room wearing their gray overcoats and carrying their gray saucer caps. Jan and Myrna were still dressing for dinner formation while the two yearlings sat down on Jan's bed.

"Has anyone asked you guys about it yet?" Jan asked.

"Of course they have," Kristi answered.

"What did you say?" Jan hadn't had a chance to speak to them before now and hoped they didn't reveal Major Behar.

"We said we could neither confirm nor deny any involvement," Pamela said.

"But surely everyone would assume you were involved anyway," Jan said while grabbing the gray scarf from her closet.

"We thought so, too, at first," Pamela said.

"Yeah, but then we heard other women in the company being asked the same question. And they answered the same way, 'we can neither confirm nor deny,'" Kristi said.

"You're kidding." Jan turned to face her friends holding her scarf around her neck. "Why the heck would they do that?"

Myrna chimed in, "They're trying to help, Jan. If all, or

even some, female cadets refuse to answer, that makes it almost impossible for anyone to find out who really is involved."

"But who told them to do that? How did they know to say the same thing as you guys?" Jan asked, disbelieving.

Pamela and Kristi shrugged. "Beats me," Kristi said.

Myrna had bent down to tie her shoelaces. "Well, I'm glad that's going to help you two," Jan said, "but I've already admitted my involvement to my CO, XO and platoon sergeant. Fortunately, I didn't mention you or anyone else's names."

Myrna stood back up. "Damn."

Jan shrugged, "The good news is that they seemed to take it well."

Jan fell in her squad line by the men's latrines at 1930 hours. The plebes had already been weighed and the yearlings were next. When Heggenbach called Jan's name, she entered the men's latrine and walked into the shower area. A scale had been placed in the middle of the white tiled room. Heggenbach sat on a chair flanking the scale, holding a clipboard on his lap. Her squad leader, Mike Miller, stood perpendicular to the base of the scale.

"Step up, Jan," Mike said.

She had worn black and gold PT shorts, her white PT shirt with the academy crest and last name over her left breast and flip-flops. She stepped out of the flip-flops, hesitated slightly and then stepped onto the scale. Mike reached around her right side to adjust the weights, placing the large weight on the 100. He moved the smaller one to 30, then to 40. When the needle on the right side of the weights remained solidly in the up position, Jan lifted her right hand and moved the big weight to the 150 position. The needle immediately dropped, making a noise as it hit the metal barrier.

"There ya go," she said.

Mike moved the smaller weight back to the 10 position.

The needle lifted slightly without leveling in the middle. Her squad leader then nudged the smaller weight slightly to the left until the needle settled at the horizontal position.

"158 pounds," he said to John Heggenbach.

"Wishart, 158 pounds," the platoon leader repeated for verification.

Neither cadet shouted. But it seemed to Jan that their voices bounced off the tiles and gained volume before echoing down the company hallway and out of the New South doors. The sound reverberated off the stone buildings and bronze statues until the entire Corps of Cadets heard: "Wishart—158 pounds!"

At Saturday morning formation, Jan fell in her squad line at the last possible minute. She heard the fourth squad leader questioning his female plebe. "Did you have anything to do with the article in *The New York Times* about women cadets, Miss Danby?"

"Sir, I can neither confirm nor deny any involvement."

Jan couldn't believe the plebe's response. She listened again as the second squad leader asked Myrna the same question. "I can neither confirm nor deny involvement," she said.

What is this?

She perked her ears and listened to the other platoons. The same question was being asked all over the company. All the squad leaders were asking the women about their involvement in *The New York Times* article. Jan heard the same answer over and over, "I can neither confirm nor deny..."

Jesus. How did that happen?

She hardly noticed Mike Miller standing in front of her. "Jan, sorry, but I have to ask, were you involved in yesterday's *New York Times* article about women cadets?"

"Why do you *have to* ask, Mike?"

"It's from the TAC. He wants all the squad leaders to ask

their female cadets about it," he replied.

Jan stared him squarely in the eyes. "I can neither confirm nor deny involvement."

NINETEEN

"Every strike brings me closer to the next home run."
(Babe Ruth)

December 12, 1982
0800 hours

She stands atop the hill surveying her victory over the gray men. They are dead. ALL DEAD.

I've killed them all, thank God.

If she hadn't, they would have killed her, she's sure of that. She begins counting the bodies.

One, two, three, four, five, six... Wait! One is moving.

She raises her hunting knife. She charges down the hill to finish that one off. The man rolls over. She knows him! It's her brother, Peter.

Oh no! What have I done?

She didn't mean to stab her own brother. What if he dies because of what she has done? She keeps running down the hill toward him. She will try to save him.

Before she can reach him, she trips over another gray body. She falls to the ground. Her head is level with the open, empty eyes of another man in gray.

It's Drew! I have killed Drew! OH MY GOD! How could I kill my best friend?

She lifts herself up and continues toward Peter.

I must save him. I must get to him.

But she can barely move. Each step is agonizingly slow. She is stuck, as if in mud.

The bells begin ringing again.

STOP! STOP IT! STOP RINGING, DAMN BELLS!

The Cadet Chapel bells won again. Jan groaned and turned over. She slowly opened her eyes expecting to see her roommate still sleeping. Instead, Myrna was gone, her bed had already been made. Jan couldn't remember one time when Myrna was out of the room before Jan.

Wonder what's up with that?

She made her own bed in less than a minute. Most cadets learned how to sleep with minimal disturbance to their sheets and blanket, thus avoiding a total remake of the bed each morning. If they were very good at it, as Jan was, they could simply fluff the pillow, tuck in the top part of the sheet and blanket and refold the Gray Girl. Only on Sundays, when they could sleep in, did Jan sometimes allow herself to indulge with the bed sheets.

But the damn bells usually ruin it for me.

She walked to the latrine, showered and returned to her room to find her mattress on the floor; sheets, blanket and Gray Girl scattered about; and the trash can upended on top of the gray metal bed frame. Its contents had fallen through the slats. Several books had been yanked from the bookshelves, resting now on her desk and the floor beneath. She looked in her mirror over the sink cabinet. Staring back at her was a crude picture of a penis next to the words, "SUCK THIS!"

This might be a good time to quit.

Jan began the old argument with herself as she put her room back in order. She listed all the reasons why she should resign from West Point while there was still time. Once the first day of classes began next year, she would no longer have the choice.

She had plenty of good reasons to leave—besides hating it, feeling totally out of place, unwanted and disrespected, there was also the fact that the uniforms did nothing to accentuate her figure.

She threw her mattress back on its rack, remade her bed quickly and then began reassembling her bookshelves.

I have more than enough reasons to leave this place. No one would blame me if I did.

Yet even as she positioned the last book in descending height order, she knew she would never leave by choice. She would stay and SHE WOULD GRADUATE from West Point. Not because she liked being a cadet or even because she wanted to be in the Army, necessarily. No, more than anything else, she would FINISH, just to prove the goddamn bastards wrong. She would win this thing.

By God, when I leave, it will be with the fucking diploma in my hands!

Jan Wishart came from a long line of obstinate souls. She might get kicked out or she might even fail out, but she would never leave by choice. She had something to prove now—to Major Stanley, to Chris Barrington, to Captain Landau, to Joey Lishiski, to the commandant's son, to all the dicks who fucked with her and Kristi, and to anyone else who didn't want women at West Point—BY GOD—she would show them.

On Sunday night, Rick joined Jan for a physics study session in Kristi and Pamela's room. He brought along his roommate, Peter Ng, who was practically a physics savant. Peter sat in Kristi's chair between the beds and rattled off hints whenever the rest got stuck on the practice problems, which happened frequently. Jan and Rick sat on Violet's bed (who was somewhere "studying" with Joey), while Pamela and Kristi sat on the lower bunk bed on the opposite wall. Several large textbooks lay open around both sets of rack-seated cadets. They were about halfway through the practice problems when an H-1 firstie stopped at their open door.

"Y'all are looking pretty serious in here," he said.

"This is serious stuff, Rivers," Pamela said. "Why don't you pull up a chair and tell us how to pass this bugger, since you must have done it once?"

The firstie walked into the room, noticed the physics textbooks and said, "Damn, I barely passed that course, can't help you much with any of that."

His politeness to his company mates melted Jan's heart just a little. "Is that your name? Rivers?" she asked.

The vanilla-haired, blue-eyed young man turned to face Jan. "Yes, ma'am."

"Ma'am? Did you just call me ma'am?"

"Yes, ma'am." He smiled, showing braces on his teeth.

Jan looked at Kristi and Pamela. "Hey, how'd you train your firsties to call you ma'am?"

"Only this one does that," Pamela said. "He's from the south so he's been raised right."

"Oh, I see." Jan looked back at the smiling braces. "Is 'Rivers a southern name then?"

"No, ma'am, my momma just liked it."

Jan was intrigued. "Did she name your brother 'Trees?' Do you have a sister named 'Mountain' or something like that?"

Braces boy laughed. "No, she named them Jane and John."

"You're kidding." Jan smiled at him again while Rick picked up his textbook, looking intently at a problem.

"I think she felt bad after naming me, so she decided to give them normal names," Rivers said.

"Well, I think you got the best one," Jan said. "Who wants 'Jane' or 'John' when you can have 'Rivers?' I wish my parents had given me a name from nature, like 'Meadow,' or 'Willow,' or..."

"Babbling Brook?" Pamela interrupted.

Everyone laughed, including Peter Ng and Rick. Jan didn't mind at all. She was too curious about the cute braces-clad southern charmer who just happened to have one of the best names on the planet.

"Stagger desks!" Major Stanley announced right before passing out the physics Term End Exam. Jan had done all she could to prepare; it was only a matter of execution at this point. She felt somewhat relieved that physics required quantifiable answers. Ever since Jan toppled him at boards, he had been sneering and scowling at her in class. She was fairly certain he would fail her if he had the chance. But she wasn't going to give him that opportunity.

Peter Ng finished first. He took his paper to the P's desk and placed it face down in a manila folder. Stanley, sitting at his desk, said, "Mr. Ng, first again. Well done."

"Thank you, sir," Peter said.

After another half hour, a slew of cadets began standing and taking their papers to the folder on the P's desk. Only Jan, Rick and three others remained. Jan knew Rick had already finished. He was simply waiting for her to finish, which she did with ten minutes to spare.

At least I beat two others.

She stood and walked to Stanley's desk. She placed the test face down in the folder, avoiding eye contact with her professor.

He glanced at her anyway. "Miss Wishart, I hope you've managed to pass this exam. If not, I'm afraid you will not pass the course."

"Sir? I had a C minus coming into exam week."

"That was before your last few class participation grades were factored in."

Shit, subjective grades.

"I'm afraid you're sitting at a D." Stanley smiled. "So failing this exam will mean you fail the course."

Dick!

She wanted to shout. Instead, she smiled at Stanley, patted the manila folder and said, "I think I did pretty well, sir."

She moved toward the door as Rick placed his exam in the folder. Jan heard him say, "She studied with Cadet Ng, sir, so she probably aced it."

To relieve tension, Jan and Rick took a mid-week afternoon run. They wore their gray USMA sweat suits, Etonic sneakers, black and gold beanie caps and black gloves to run Thayer Road to Thayer Gate and back.

Jan thought the bleak, cold grayness of mid-winter was the best time to run at West Point. The white snow outlined the stone buildings, the cannons and the statues, allowing hidden details to be seen. Eisenhower's tie, the bridle on Washington's horse, the binoculars in Patton's hands and the coat draped on MacArthur's arm revealed the subtle beauty of West Point.

"Hey, I didn't really say thank you for waiting for me during the physics exam," Jan said.

"I didn't want you to be the last one there with Major Stanley...turns out I didn't need to stay, though."

"But I'm glad you did. And I'm glad you said something about me studying with Ng. That ought to make him think twice about failing me."

"Jan, he can fail you for class participation—that's his judgment—but the exam is fairly objective," Rick said.

"Unless he wanted to change my answers."

"He's not that stupid. It's not worth risking his career."

"I hope not. I just never know with these jerks..."

Rick sighed. "Jan, not everyone here is an asshole, contrary to your opinion."

She paused before saying, "You're right. There's you and Peter. Oh, and Captain Hasuko is a nice guy."

He stopped running while she kept going for a few paces. She stopped, too, and turned around to face him. "What?"

"Jan, c'mon, what about your CO, XO and platoon sergeant who prayed for you and vowed to keep you safe?"

"What about them? It was probably all for show, so they can feign innocence when I'm found dead in the men's latrine." She knew she was overreacting, but she also needed to vent. She needed someone to hear her anger.

"Jan, what are you talking about? No one is out to kill you. Yes, there are some jerks who are trying to get under your skin, but no one's waiting in the dark to stab you with a knife!"

The words seem to hang in the cold air. Jan felt them linger in front of her face before seeming to explode up her nose. He had made a direct reference to what happened last year in the darkness of Washington Hall. Was he insinuating that she and Kristi were guilty of premeditation? Jan felt her eyes sting.

She began shouting, "What the hell is that supposed to mean, Rick? You think Kristi and I planned what happened last year? You think we waited in the dark to ambush him? Huh? IS that what you think, Rick?" She felt her face flush hotly and her temples throb. "Well, fuck you, Rick! Fuck you! And every goddamn asshole in this place!"

"Geez, Jan, I'm only saying that not every one is the freaking enemy! Sometimes it seems like you hate everyone and everything! I just don't think you have to be like that all the time." He seemed to be pleading.

"Well, Rick, try walking in my boots for a while...you might see why I feel that way. It's a goddamn war zone everyday for most of us. You have the luxury of being a man, Rick, which makes your life here at least half as hard as ours." Then, because she was really pissed off, she added, "At least, I think you're a man."

Oh shit! No, I didn't mean that.

They stared at each other for a long moment. Jan tried to say "sorry," but her throat felt like it had frozen shut. Apologizing, admitting wrongdoing, was never her strong suit. And it wouldn't happen now, even though it needed to.

Then, turning on his Etonics, Rick ran ahead of her back to the barracks.

She walked slowly back knowing she may have lost the only male friend she had left at West Point. And she began to realize there was something wrong with her. Deep inside, something was broken, or it never worked in the first place, or maybe it was just plain missing.

I'm fucked up. That's the problem. Plain and simple.

TWENTY

"Upon the fields of friendly strife are sown the seeds that upon other fields, on other days, will bear the fruits of victory."
(General Douglas MacArthur, USMA Class of 1903)

December 17, 1982
0015 hours

On Friday of TEE week, Jan barged into Kristi and Pamela's room after Taps and asked, "Shall we celebrate?" Even though they had finished their last Term End Exam, no one could leave until all exams ended on Saturday. At that point, the entire Corps of Cadets would file out of West Point faster than the water that rushes over the spillway in Lusk Reservoir.

Celebratory options were severely limited. As upperclassmen, they could go to Ike Hall for a beer and bad pizza, or to Grant Hall for an ice cream, or to any of the academic areas—library, computer room or other cadet rooms. They could always go to the gym or for a run. Or they could break the rules and go wherever the hell they wanted.

"Kristi and I were planning to go on an adventure with a few of the firsties in our company, I'm sure they won't mind one more," Pamela said.

"Where you going?" Jan asked.

"I'm not sure, some bar probably." The drinking age was eighteen but rumors of it being raised caused cadets to feel even more anxious to drink as often as possible while they could.

"Okay, I'm in, let me just go unmark my card." She turned toward the door. "Be right back."

They ended up at the Boiler Room Pub in Newburgh, NY, about thirty minutes outside Post. The bar was mostly empty, except for a few locals. Kristi, Jan, Pamela and the three firsties from H-1, Crigger, Moe and Rivers sat at a small round table holding six mugs of beer. Unlike Rivers, Crigger was actually a nickname; his given name was Christopher.

After some small talk, Jan asked, "Hey, what do you guys know about your classmate, John Heggenbach?"

"He's a good dude," Moe said. "A bit of a Strac-master, though." "Strac" meant someone who did everything according to regulations, a cadet who never crossed the lines.

"His ass is harder than this table top," Crigger added.

Jan smiled thinking that she was the only one who actually knew that for sure. She also realized John Heggenbach wasn't someone she would ever get close to. He wasn't going to be boyfriend material. Hell, he might not even be her friend. She decided it was best to forget what happened at Army/Navy and move on.

"Why'd you ask?" Rivers asked.

"Oh, just curious, that's all. He's my platoon sergeant this semester."

They crammed into the car for the return ride back to Post. Moe drove, with Crigger on the passenger side and Kristi in between them. Pamela sat behind Moe, Jan in the middle and Rivers on her right. Although Jan had been flirting with Rivers, he wasn't taking the bait. In the car, she decided to be more demonstrative. When Moe made left turns, Jan leaned farther to the right than was necessary, just for effect. On a particularly sharp curve, she practically fell into his lap.

Oops!

Finally, he got the message and placed his hand on her leg, helping to stabilize the poor thing. Her plan was working.

They returned to Post about 0315 hours. Sneaking back into the barracks was sometimes trickier than sneaking out. They parked the car in the lot above Michie Stadium and made the downhill trek to the Cadet Chapel, staying off the roads to avoid being seen. Once at the chapel, they descended the long stairway leading to the access road behind the mess hall. Using the cover of darkness, they quietly slipped up the side ramp to New South. Crigger approached the heavy wooden doors first and gave the hand signal showing "all clear." The other five cadets ran in and up the stairs. Jan peeled off at the second floor. Rivers followed.

Jan quietly opened the door to her room. She saw Myrna asleep in her rack. She gently closed the door, turned around and whispered, "My roommate's asleep and she'll wake up if we go in."

Because her room was located down a small hallway off the main hallway, they had some measure of privacy. So they began making out. Heavily. Rivers seemed like a starving child who hadn't eaten in days. He couldn't get enough of kissing Jan.

He's not quite as shy as I thought.

She felt like he would devour her. "Whoa, whoa there, cowboy," she whispered. "Save a little for next time."

"When?" he asked, still chewing on her lip.

"When, what?"

"When's next time?"

"I don't know, but we have to stop here for now. I can't bring you in my room with sleeping beauty in there."

"Okay, okay...but...definitely want to do this again, okay?" He said while still nibbling on parts of her face.

"Okay." She didn't mind if they reprised things sometime down the road. She would be happy to swim the Rivers in the future.

"Soon, okay." He couldn't seem to pull away.

"Okay, Rivers, yes, okay." She didn't really want to end it either but they were pushing their luck already. "You have to let me go now, Rivers."

"What the hell is going on here?" John Heggenbach seemed to come out of the wall.

Jan and Rivers pulled apart quickly. "He's just walking me to my room," Jan blurted out without thinking.

"At almost 0400 hours?" Heggenbach folded his arms across his chest.

Rivers tried to smooth it over. "Wow! That late? Already? We really lost track of time. Guess I better get going..."

"What were you two doing?" John asked.

"We were talking, John," Rivers said, which was the truth.

"And what else?" John asked.

Neither Jan nor Rivers answered. They just stood by her door dumbfounded by the question.

How dare he get on his high horseback?

"Far less than what you did a few weeks back," she blurted out.

Heggenbach seemed stunned. He shifted his weight from one foot to the other. Jan knew she had something on him now. He couldn't deny it without violating the Honor Code. He might not want it widely known, either.

Maybe I have the upper handle for once.

"Look, I'm going to my room now. If you want to make something of this, you know where to find me, John." Rivers pushed past the G-1 firstie. "Night, Jan," he said as he headed back to his room in H-1.

Heggenbach stood in the hallway staring at Jan. "I thought you were better than this, Jan."

She stared right back. "Better than what, John?"

"This!" His face contorted. "Screwing around."

"I wasn't screwing around, John. In fact, I've only screwed around with you, if you must know."

"Sure looks like you were about to," he said with pursed lips.

"Well, I wasn't. But it's none of your business, anyway. I don't have to report in to you about my love life."

"No, you don't, but you might want to think about your reputation when you're hanging around with guys all the time."

"What?" Jan gaped at him. "I live in the world's largest frat house, John, how am I supposed to avoid hanging around with guys?"

"You know what I mean," he said.

"No, John, I DON'T know what you mean. What the hell DO you mean, exactly?" She felt the redness rising again.

But he didn't answer. After a long pause, he turned around and walked back to his room.

TWENTY-ONE

All I was doing was trying to get home from work.
(Rosa Parks)

December 20, 1982
1245 hours

Jan awoke to see her mother standing just inside the door of her own room, in her own home, in her own great state of New Hampshire.

"Jan, it's Kristi," Mrs. Wishart whispered while holding the receiver of the telephone in one hand and cupping the mouthpiece with her other hand. "Do you want me to tell her to call back?"

"Naw, I'll take it." Jan crawled out of bed. "Thanks, Ma," she mumbled, taking the phone from her mother. She turned her back to the doorframe, sliding down it until she sat cross-legged just inside her room. The cord stretched from the receiver all the way down the hallway to its base, which hung on the wall at the entrance to the kitchen.

For Jan, going home was almost a spiritual event. Not just because of sleeping in her old bed, nor her mom's Sunday pot roast, nor even the family dog that licked her face like she had come home from war. It was the feeling of safety more than anything, which made going home so damn great. Jan knew she could lie, cheat, steal, screw, fail, scream, get fat, get drunk, get fucking pissed off—and still not get kicked out. She began to understand—perhaps, for the first time—the meaning of "family."

"Hey," Jan managed to get out.

"You sound perky." Kristi's voice actually felt comforting. As much as they sometimes tired of each other, West Point friends became your extended family—they knew all about you and didn't mind at all.

"Yeah, well, you just woke me up," Jan said groggily.

"Oh, sorry about that. Well, you need to get up anyway and go for a run, right?"

"Shit, yeah." Of course, Jan would *not* go for a run. Not during the first two weeks of Christmas leave.

"Well, Pamela and I have been talking..."

Kristi had spent one week of Christmas leave with her family in Germany, before flying to Texas to spend the next week at Pamela's house and was supposed to spend the last week with Jan before returning to West Point for second semester. Jan assumed Kristi never stayed in one place too long because she grew up as a diplomat's daughter, moving every few years.

Kristi continued, "We think it would be really great if we *both* came to your house next week, then the three of us can visit Drew before we have to report back to prison."

"Does Pamela want to do that?" Jan doubted Pamela would want that much togetherness.

"Yup. She's getting bored, too."

Of the three, only Jan seemed to crave more, not less, time at home. "Okay, whatever works for you guys." At least they weren't cancelling, she thought. "So will you two be on the same flight, then?"

"Yeah, I'll call the day before. Hey, what's the plan for

New Year's?"

Last year, Jan and Kristi went to Jan's ex-boyfriend's New Year's Eve party, held on the porch and in the large yard behind his house. Wood fires in fifty-five gallon drums and a central bonfire kept everyone warm. It was the best party in her small New Hampshire town, although it was a little awkward for Jan.

"I don't know. Maybe we'll just stay here and get drunk this year. It's the same thing, only in a different place."

"That sounds good," Kristi said. It was always about getting drunk. Not much else mattered.

Jan shared almost everything with Kristi and Pamela, but in her journal, she expressed her deepest fears and emotions. The entries became a little darker, a little sadder and a little lonelier each time. Three days before Kristi and Pamela arrived, she wrote:

I'm glad my girls are coming soon. That way, I will have an excuse to actually get out of bed. I've been sleeping most of the time since I've been home. I didn't even get out of my pajamas for a few days. Mom is beginning to get worried; she keeps asking me if I have the blues.

The "blues?"

I have the fucking "blacks," Mom! I can't see a fucking thing! The lights are out! The only relief from the goddamn darkness is drinking and sleeping!

Jan believed in God—a benevolent God. One who looked down on the world and occasionally helped people if they were very good. Her version of God would not help bad people, and since Jan was turning more and more to the dark side, she figured God wasn't likely to do much for her.

Still, she prayed. She prayed a lot. She prayed all the time:

God, I know I don't deserve anything. But if you have some time, can you help me figure things out?

God, I know you have a lot more important things on your plate. But when you get a minute, can you help me get through this day, this week, okay this whole year?

God, I haven't been a great person, I know. I think I am beginning to hate a lot of people—particularly those of the male sex. I know some men are probably very nice so I am trying to keep an open mind. If you can help me out here, I promise to be a better person. I promise to be nicer to my family, especially my younger sister. I promise to try to do more to help others. I just need a little help myself right now.

Jan's God only loved the good and kind people. Her God only helped those who did good deeds. She believed in a Banker God—one who paid interest only after a deposit had been made. And she was always overdrawn.

The phone rang again later that night. Jan picked up the receiver. "Hello?"

"Hey...Jan."

"Hey...who is this?"

"John."

"John?"

"Hegg-en-bach."

"Oh, hi...John." He was the last person she expected to hear from.

"I was juss thinkin'...and thought I'd...call," he slurred the words.

"Well, that's...nice."

A long paused ensued.

"Yeah. I was...(sigh), ...shit..."

"Are you okay, John?"

"Yeah, I'm fine. Is juss...Well, guess tha's it, then."

"That's what?"

"Tha's...tha' it?"

"What do you mean, John?"

"I mean me. An' you."

"I don't know what you mean."

After another long pause, she said, "We should talk when you're sober."

"DAMMIT!"

"John, I don't know what you want."

"Yes, you do. You know eggs-zac-ly wha' I wan."

Jan felt her neck go red. Her temples began throbbing. John Heggenbach might become her company commander next semester; he could be in her direct chain of command; or his room could end up right next to hers. There were many ways he could make her life a living hell for the next five months.

Yet she could not let him go unanswered. She had to stand up for herself. *Remember what Jean Rallins said: Show no fear.*

"John, you're drunk. And because you are drunk, I am going to excuse what I think you just said. But let's be clear about one thing: you and I are not going to be together again! It only happened that one time because we were both drunk. And stupid. Otherwise, I can assure you, it would not have taken place."

The third long pause followed.

"Wishart, you know what?"

"What? Hegg-en-bach!"

"I'm drunk. And 'cuz I'm drunk, I'm gonna scuse what I think you juss said." She heard him spit or something. "But less be clear about one ting: you and I are gonna...prob-ly, anyway. It only happens one time because we were bof drunk and stu-pi. So..I can 'sure you, it will...i's bound to happen...again."

Then he hung up.

On New Year's Eve, the trio drank Mogen David wine until the Times Square ball dropped on television. Then they went to bed. Anti-climactic. They spent the next couple of days drinking, eating, sleeping and then going running—to relieve the guilt for drinking, eating and sleeping.

Mr. Wishart dropped them, hungover, at the Greyhound station for the bus ride to NYC. They slept almost the whole way. When they arrived at Grand Central Station, Drew greeted them in his usual impeccable clothing. This would be their last hurrah before having to report back to their gray cells.

They ordered pizza and beer at the same place as their last visit to Drew's. "What happened when they questioned you about the article?" he asked.

"Well, at first I confessed to my CO, XO and platoon sergeant," Jan said. "I wish I had thought to say the 'neither confirm nor deny' phrase."

Kristi added, "but you only told those three guys, who all seem to be on your side."

"Yeah, we'll see about that. I don't trust at least one of them," Jan added.

"Well, we seem to be out of the woods for now," Pamela said. "Somehow all the other women answered the same way, neither confirming nor denying involvement. Someone was looking out for us, that's for sure."

Drew sighed deeply, seemingly relieved that his three friends had avoided a backlash. He knew it could have been much worse. "I didn't expect Steve Calibrio to mention where he got his information. Next time, I will be sure he doesn't say anything about 'Gals in Gray.'"

"Next time?" Jan asked.

"Well, yeah, Jan. There will be follow-up articles. The response has been huge and Steve is probably going to do interviews with some of the women who have left."

"Fine, I just don't want to have anything more to do with it," Jan said.

"But, Jan," Drew said, "you three are the only ones on the inside who can tell us what's really going on."

Kristi spoke up. "Jan's right, we need to let things cool down a while. It's too explosive for us right now."

"My vote is always with my girls," Pamela added.

"Sorry, Drew, but if one more thing even smells like it came from us, we might be on the outside too," Jan added.

Drew agreed they were right and said he didn't want to jeopardize their status anymore than necessary. "I understand you want to keep a low profile for a while. Okay, I get it. But promise me one thing?"

"What?"

"If something big happens, will you let me know?"

"What do you mean by 'big?'" Kristi asked.

"You'll know when it happens," he said.

Jan, Kristi and Pamela stared at Drew wondering if he knew something they didn't.

TWENTY-TWO

"You have to do your own growing no matter how tall your grandfather was."
(Abraham Lincoln)

January 9, 1983
1530 hours

Jan read the new room and chain of command lists for second semester on the company bulletin board.

Shit.

She would have to swap rooms with Lisa Techtton. Leslie, Esther and Myrna didn't have to lift a finger—those three women didn't have to change rooms. To make matters worse, Myrna had been assigned as Jan's new squad leader and John Heggenbach had been named as G-1's new company commander.

Shit again!

She stormed back to her room where she stuffed as much as possible into one of her big black trunks. While holding the leather strap at one end, she dragged it through the hallway to room 215.

Most everyone else was doing the same thing. The

hallways across the Corps filled with cadets moving their trunks and duffel bags full of uniforms, books and Gray Girls. Plebes had it worse, having to transport everything while staying along the walls and squaring the corners of the building. God help the beanheads who had to go up or down stairs.

Jan fumed that three women in G-1 got to sit on their asses while everyone else lugged their shit to new rooms. This was another example of bad publicity, she thought. No one liked "get overs," especially women "get overs." Pushing her heavy trunk down the hallway, Jan felt slightly better knowing she was not one of them.

Dogety would be proud of me.

Jan continued to measure herself in the eyes of her Beast squad leader from last year. She wondered if she would ever be out from under the burden of his gaze—which was now only in her imagination.

She finished putting her room in order by 1900 hours and hustled upstairs to visit Kristi, Pamela and Violet, who all remained roommates but still had to move rooms. Company H-1, anyway, seemed to understand the importance of making everyone move.

"Well, at least we're all at the same end of the hallway this semester," Jan said as she walked through their door. "Takes about half as long to get to your room."

"Does that mean we'll see you twice as often?" Pamela asked, while still arranging her bookshelf.

"Only if you're very lucky." Jan smiled.

Kristi stood near her underwear drawer, folding bras and panties. "Speaking of lucky, guess who's our next door neighbor this semester?" she asked.

Jan glanced around the room, making sure Violet was not around. "Um, hopefully not Joey Lishiski." Her friends would never get any sleep if Violet's boyfriend lived next door.

Kristi held up a bra and waved it at Jan. "Rivers Preston," she said in a sing-song voice.

"Oh, that's great. You guys will get to see him all the time, then." Jan felt a pang of jealousy.

"He'll probably only stop by whenever you're here, Jan." Pamela winked at her.

"I don't know, Pam, I'm not sure he even remembers that..."

"Knock, knock." Rivers stood in the hallway outside their room, wearing jeans and an Army rugby t-shirt.

"Speak of the devil," Pamela whispered.

Jan froze in Kristi's desk chair feeling unsure of what to say or do. She hadn't seen Rivers since the last hurried encounter outside her room after Taps.

"May I come in, ladies?" He sauntered into the room, not waiting for permission.

"Sure, Rivers, you're always welcome in our abode," Pamela said.

Jan pretended to read something on Kristi's desk while Rivers walked straight toward her. He stopped at the windowsill and turned to face the interior of the room, between Jan and Pamela. He crossed his arms and leaned against the sill, looking comfortable and casual. She felt a familiar shiver run through her legs.

"Hey, Jan, how's it going?" he asked.

Jan looked toward him while avoiding eye contact. "Going fine, Rivers. You?"

"I'm good, thanks." He looked toward Pamela, who suddenly stopped arranging her bookshelf and walked to the sink counter, loading her toiletries into the mirrored cabinet. Kristi became even more engrossed in organizing her underwear drawer.

In a quieter tone, Rivers turned back to Jan. "Just wondered if you'd like to get together again sometime."

Ah, so he did remember. "Get together? Whatever do you mean by that?" She smiled to let him know she was teasing.

Rivers threw his head back and laughed, showing his full

set of braces. "Whatever it means to you is fine with me."

After a year and a half at West Point surrounded by approximately four thousand guys, this was the first time one had asked her out. At least that's what she thought he was doing.

"Sure, I'd be happy to *get together* sometime." She smiled at him. "Preferably not right outside *my room,* however."

His head tilted back again as he laughed through his braces. Jan could see the remnants of the little boy he once was—innocent, carefree and unself-conscious—as he leaned against the windowsill, left foot over right and arms folded across his chest.

Second semester began with the usual "back to the grindstone" enthusiasm among the Corps. With the grayness of winter hovering over the gray buildings and the gray cadets, it was always a small miracle when no major catastrophes occurred. This was the most likely season for a firstie to drive his car into a tree, or for a plastered cow to fall from atop Washington's statue, or for a plebe to be found asleep in a laundry cart.

Jan soon discovered that she had the room to herself most of the time. Leslie was always at practice or matches with the tennis team, and Esther was almost always with her boyfriend, supposedly at the library, computer room, or Grant Hall. Jan knew they were often not at any of those places, but somewhere else having sex. Esther was very open about it, telling Jan where they went and even how they did it.

It was still an enigma to Jan why everyone seemed to think sex was so great. Esther assured her it was indeed wonderful "if the guy knows what to do."

"What, exactly, should the guy know?" Jan asked.

"You know," she paused before adding, "he should know how to touch you."

Oh, that explains everything.

"So, how should he?" She turned to face Esther. "How should he...touch you?"

"Jan!" For the first time, Esther seemed a little embarrassed.

"What? I want to know what you mean, Esther."

"Haven't you ever touched yourself?" she asked.

Is that normal? "Like, do you mean...well, I'm not sure what you mean."

"God, Jan! You haven't, have you?"

"Haven't what? It might help if I knew what the hell you were talking about."

"Orgasm, Jan, OR-GAZ-EM!"

Jan was raised as a good lapsed-Catholic girl. She didn't "touch herself"—that was sinful—wasn't it? And besides, it's not like she ever had any reason to. She played softball, field hockey and basketball. She partied and hung out with friends. She wasn't a loser/loner who sat home and "touched herself," which is what she thought of those who did.

Yet she felt embarrassed to be in the dark on this. Obviously, she lacked a great deal of sexual knowledge. She hadn't read up on it either, not even sure where or how she could ever have procured a book on the subject in her small hometown. She decided it was best to admit ignorance and hope Esther would provide some vital information.

"Well, I'm not really sure what that is, actually." There, she said it.

"Oh, Jan, Jan, Jan." Esther shook her head.

Jan thought of the television show, *The Brady Bunch*, where the middle daughter, Jan, often said to her older sister, "Marcia, Marcia, Marcia."

"You have no idea what you're missing, do you, Jan?" Esther asked.

"Well, if I did, I don't suppose I'd be asking you now, would I?" Jan felt like an idiot. But the payoff might be big, she figured, making it all worth it.

"Okay, that's it, I'm going to lend you my book. I'll get it next time I go home. It will tell you everything you need to know."

Esther was from New York City and a voracious reader, so it came as no surprise that she would have a book on sex. "Okay," Jan said, hoping this would be the last time she would ever have an embarrassing conversation on the subject.

"I'd like you to be there with me," she said to John Heggenbach, her new CO. Jan had just asked him to accompany her to the TAC's office.

"I don't think you need me for that, Jan," he said.

"Maybe not. But I'd feel more comfortable if you came along. Remember how he treated me last time I went to him?" John didn't respond. "About the diet tables?" When he remained silent again, she added, "Please."

"Okay, let's go." He followed her to the TAC's office on the first floor.

Captain Landau sat behind his desk reading papers when Jan approached the open door. She knocked twice. "Enter," he said without looking up.

She walked to the front of his desk, stopping about three feet away. Saluting, she said, "sir, Cadet Wishart reporting to make a statement."

She held the salute until Captain Landau looked up briefly, giving the customary return salute. "What is it now, Miss Wishart?"

She could feel John Heggenbach's presence beside her. "Sir, my Gray Girl has been vandalized."

Captain Landau kept looking at his papers. "And?"

"And, sir, I thought I should report it to you."

Captain Landau stopped reading and looked up at Jan for the first time. "Pranks happen all the time, Miss Wishart. I'm not sure it rises to the level of vandalism."

"Sir, someone used cigarettes to burn my name and a big

"X" over it."

"When did this happen?"

"Mid-November, sir."

"And you're just reporting it now?"

"Yes, sir."

He let out a long sigh. "And do you still have the Gray Girl?"

Shit.

"No, sir. I threw it out and bought a new one since it was ruined. But at least three others saw it."

"Well, Miss Wishart, the bottom line is you don't have any evidence to *show me.*" He paused again before letting out a breath. "Have there been any other incidents since then?"

"Yes, sir."

"What were they?"

"Sir, my room was torn apart on the Sunday before TEE week."

"And you didn't report that to anyone either?"

"No, sir."

"So," he interlaced his fingers, "what are you expecting me to do at this point, without any evidence and after the fact?"

"I just wanted to make you aware that it happened, sir."

"Mission accomplished, Miss Wishart. Dismissed." He saluted without waiting for her. She executed an about face and marched out of the office.

She heard John Heggenbach following behind. "Jan."

She turned to face him. "What?"

He closed the distance between them. "You did the right thing. Now he knows about it. If something else happens, he won't be able to say he didn't know anything."

She stared at him. "John, I was hoping he would *DO* something to ensure nothing else will happen."

"What can he do, really, at this point?"

Jan rolled her eyes. "First of all, he could have expressed *SOME* concern for me, he could have said *SOMETHING* like, 'I'm sorry this happened, Miss Wishart.' Secondly, he could've offered to speak to the company and say something like 'these kinds of things will *not* be tolerated in G-1.'"

"Yeah, he could've done all that, but he's not really the one who should do that."

"Well then, who should, John?"

"Me. I'm the CO. I'll do it."

She stared at him a bit longer, thinking about the difference between "sober-John" and "drunk-John." "Okay, I would appreciate that."

He looked around the hallway before saying, "And I'm very sorry that happened to you."

She wondered why he had to check the area first. Still, he was the first and perhaps the only person who apologized for the incidents.

Team Handball practice continued every afternoon during the non-parade season, which suited Jan just fine. It gave her the opportunity to exercise, improve her skills and socialize with teammates. More than anything, it supplied the needed diversion from academics, roommates, G-1, John Heggenbach and Rick Davidson.

Jan averted her eyes from the men's team practicing on the other end of the court. She didn't want to see Rick. More importantly, she didn't want him to see her watching him. She had made up her mind—she would develop the blossoming relationship with Rivers and just forget about Rick.

Yet she still felt something, she wasn't sure what, every time she thought about him. It seemed they were always either on the verge of dating or not speaking.

I just wish we could be friends again.

She told herself this lie from time to time and it seemed to pacify things.

Captain Hasuko dismissed the team after practice adding,

"Miss Wishart, please stand fast."

Jan waited near the bleachers while the rest of the team ran toward the main doors of the sixth floor gymnasium. She stole a glance at the men's team still running half court sprints and saw Rick win almost all of them.

"Miss Wishart, please sit down." Hasuko, already sitting on the bottom bleacher, patted the bench beside him.

Jan sat facing her coach. "Yes, sir?"

Hasuko looked across the gym at the exit door, ensuring the rest of the team had left. "I wanted to share something with you concerning Cadet Wan. I know you wanted to hear her story as much as I did."

"Why didn't she show up to the panel in DC, sir?"

"She reported the next day—to an empty room. She then called Jurgensen and he told her she must have misheard the date." Hasuko sighed and redirected his eyes to Jan. "She had written down the date he originally had given her—and she's positive he said Sunday, not Saturday."

"So he intentionally gave her the wrong day?"

"Possibly. Or she could have misheard him."

"Sir, my friends think the comm's assistant ordered Jurgensen to keep her away from the panel."

"I wouldn't be surprised. Her case involved the commandant's son, as you know."

"Yes, sir," Jan said. "I also heard she resigned after being charged with an Honor violation that she knew she couldn't beat." Jan thought about how she never thought she'd win her own Honor Board last year.

"That's right," Hasuko said, "and now she regrets not fighting back more." He looked back at the gym door. "I wanted you to know," he glanced around again, "Cadet Wan has talked to *The New York Times* reporter who wrote the article about women cadets. Do you know him?"

"No, sir." She paused. "But he's a friend of a friend."

"I see. Well, I just wanted to prepare you. Her story is

going to be published sometime in the next few weeks. I'm afraid it might mean more trouble for you."

"Yes, sir, it most likely will." She stood. "But I'm starting to get used to it."

Hasuko stood also, his full height stopping at the level of her neck. "Just keep the faith, Jan."

"Yes, sir."

TWENTY-THREE

Covert action should not be confused with missionary work.
(Henry A. Kissinger)

January 28, 1983
1700 hours

Jan ran straight to Kristi and Pamela's room after practice to report the latest news from Captain Hasuko. They all hoped that this new article, whenever it came out, would not mention inside sources like the "Gals in Gray."

When Jan opened the door to leave, Violet ran into the room, jumped on her bed, pulled her Gray Girl over her head, and began sobbing.

Jan shot a quizzical look at Pamela and Kristi. "What's this?" she mouthed.

Kristi shrugged her shoulders. Pamela asked, "Violet, what's wrong?"

Jan noticed that Violet had started to look thin again. She was entering her skinny phase for the second time since August.

The trio stared at each other while waiting for Violet to say something. Finally, Violet whimpered from inside her cocoon,

"I'm ruined!"

"What do you mean, Violet?" Pamela asked softly.

To everyone's astonishment, Violet shouted, "I'm fucking ruined!" This was the first time they had heard her use the "F" word.

Pamela, being the most compassionate of the trio, sat down next to her on the bed, touching her legs. "Hey, what's going on?"

Violet only continued to sob. Loudly. Jan, realizing the door had been left open, closed it before sitting down in Violet's chair. She glanced at Kristi, wondering what the heck happened to warrant such despair.

Jan finally spoke. "Vy, we're here for you. Why don't you tell us what's wrong?"

Violet abruptly lifted her Gray Girl off her head and bolted upright. "I'm fucking ruined! And there's not a goddamn thing anyone can do about it!" She slammed back down on the rack, pulling the Gray Girl over her head again.

Jan stood up. She mouthed to Kristi and Pamela, "I should go."

The wide-eyed roommates shook their heads back and forth, mouthing, "NO, STAY."

Pamela reached over, touching Violet's arm hidden somewhere under her comforter. "Vy, c'mon, tell us what's wrong." she whispered.

Silence hovered over the room as three women waited for the fourth to say something—anything. Finally, like a child who had been locked in a closet, Violet slowly lowered her Gray Girl and revealed her red, tear-streaked face. Speaking like that wounded child, she croaked, "He made a videotape."

Jan, Pamela and Kristi exchanged confused glances. "What do you mean, Vy?" Kristi asked.

"Joey," she hesitated again, "he taped us having sex."

Jan couldn't think of one person who owned a video camera, but she knew the cumbersome machines had to be set up—as on a tripod—then someone had to hit the "record" button before jumping into the picture frame. In other words, Jan was pretty sure Violet had to know she was being recorded.

"Wait, Violet." Jan paused to check her wording. "Did you *know* Joey was recording your—your—event?"

"Yes," she began wailing again, "but I never thought anyone else would see it."

"Jaysus, Mary and Joseph, Violet!" Jan shouted. "What the hell were you thinking?"

Violet began hyperventilating.

"Great, Jan, way to smooth things over." Pamela furrowed her brow.

Kristi opened her closet door and pulled the cloth cover off her black plastic plumed hat—better known as the "tar bucket." She placed the soft bag around Violet's mouth. "Take a deep breath, Vy. There, easy does it. Slow down."

With the black felt bag expanding and collapsing, Violet's breath began to normalize.

"Sorry, Violet," Jan said. "I just can't understand why you'd let him...do that."

Pamela glared at Jan again before speaking. "Honey, it's okay. You're not the first nor the last woman to have that happen."

Violet continued to cry softly. "I'm probably the first *cadet* woman, though."

Kristi said, "Great, that means you'll go down in history." Jan smirked at Kristi while Pamela frowned at both of them.

"His roommates found it and watched it—and now he's agreed to let them show it to all their friends."

"Oh no, he didn't!" Kristi objected.

"Like hell, he will!" Pamela echoed.

"Yeah, we'll steal it first," Jan said, forgetting the Honor Code for a moment. "Oh, wait, that won't work, will it?"

"I'm ruined," Violet continued to weep, "he's showing it tonight in the dayroom!"

"SHIT! SHIT! SHIT!" The trio exclaimed all at once.

"We've got to think of something. FAST!" Pamela looked at Jan.

"Don't look at me," Jan protested.

Kristi started pacing the room while Pamela pulled the regulations manual off her shelf.

"Maybe..." Pamela talked while leafing through the thick three-ring binder. "Maybe there's a rule about home videos—maybe they aren't allowed..."

Jan stared out the window, trance-like, still wondering why anyone in their right mind would allow themselves to be taped having sex.

Kristi stopped pacing. "I have an idea!" They all turned to her, including Violet. "We'll distract them while one of us 'borrows' it."

Pamela closed the regulations binder. "You mean we'll steal it?"

"No, we'll borrow it," Kristi reiterated. "Besides, it's technically Violet's tape...she has the rights to it, right?"

"What the hell, Kissy?" Jan didn't want to participate in any antics that might result in more Area tours—or worse. "The last thing we need is anything that smacks of an Honor violation."

"C'mon, Jan, let's hear her plan," Pamela said. "You'd want us to do something if it was your sex tape, right?"

Like that's ever going to happen. Yet she knew that they had to do something. It would have been unconscionable not to try to stop the viewing of the videotape, at the very least.

"Okay, let's hear it, Kissy."

Violet's crying calmed down to merely sniffling while Kristi explained her plan. After hearing the details, Violet said, "Guys, this will never work."

"I think it's brilliant," Pamela chimed in. "Besides, it's our only option."

"Well, we do have other options," Jan offered. "For

instance, we could confront Joey and tell him to hand over the freaking sex tape."

"I've already begged him for it," Violet said. "He says since his roommates have seen it, everyone else might as well see it."

"That's horseshit," Kristi exclaimed.

"He's an exemplary officer and a gentleman," Jan stated matter of factly.

Pamela winced. "Guys, you're not helping."

"Okay, let's steal it then," Jan's anger had risen to the brazen boldness point.

"You mean, borrow it," Kristi added.

"Whatever. Let's just get the fucking fucking-tape away from those bastards." Jan knew in that moment that they would settle for nothing less than victory.

They all agreed that Violet did have the rights to the videotape since she was one of the main actors. Therefore, their plan would not violate the Honor Code.

In addition, Pamela reminded them that videotapes were considered public property in the battalion. Companies often borrowed and exchanged movies. For instance, Company G-1 might borrow *Caddyshack* from Company H-1, and Company I-1 might borrow *Animal House* from Company G-1. It was considered perfectly normal for a videotape to circulate in all three companies until everyone forgot which company it actually belonged to.

"Also," Pamela said, "it's highly unlikely anyone's going to ask about it once it goes missing."

Just after Taps, the four women met in the G-1 dayroom, dressed in their gray USMA sweat suits. They could hear the men gathering in the H-1 dayroom across the basement hallway. Masculine sounds of high-fives, wrestling, butt-slapping, "hu-ahh" and raucous laughter only served to make them even more determined to go through with the plan. Still, a shiver ran down Jan's spine thinking about what they were about to do.

They heard the H-1 dayroom door close. Kristi peeked out the G-1 door, confirming that all males had entered the den of iniquity. The four women casually walked into the hallway. Jan, Kristi and Pamela continued toward the stairwell while Violet remained near the Coke machine. Her role was to loiter there until she heard the signal.

The three other women ran up the steps and out the main doors. They kept running around the short side of the building, coming to a halt halfway behind their barracks. A small pathway separated the stone exterior and the woods leading uphill to the water tower.

It was just enough room.

The G and I companies' dayrooms, located on the front side of the building, had small, high windows on the outside wall facing the courtyard. The H-1 dayroom, located on the backside of the building, had its high windows just above the path, facing the wooded hill.

The three friends crouched on the path, peering into the H-1 windows. The assembled cadets sat on several rows of worn-out couches with their backs toward the trio outside. Jan recognized a few heads and was pleased to see that Rivers wasn't one of them. On the opposite wall, just to the right of the main door, Joey Lishiski's roommate pushed a tape into the VCR player. A large television mounted on the wall above him came to life.

The three women held their breath when the roommate turned around, seemingly looking right at them, before he took a seat on the front row.

The tape began to play. Jan saw Violet in her bra and underwear walking around a room. She saw Violet flop on a bed, her mouth moving, saying something the three friends could not hear. Then Violet took one of the bra straps off one shoulder.

"Now!" Kristi whisper shouted.

Simultaneously, Kristi and Pamela lifted their gray USMA sweatshirts, while Jan lowered her gray sweatpants. None of them wore undergarments. Jan turned around and splayed her butt on the middle window, banging her fists against the glass on either side. Kristi and Pamela, wearing their black ski masks with eye and mouth holes, pressed their breasts against the windows to Jan's left and right while also banging against the glass.

The rows of seated men jerked their heads to see the commotion coming from behind them. When they saw the *live* pornography, they quickly abandoned the taped version and jumped over the couches, tripping over each other on their way to the back wall.

Jan began gyrating her butt in circles, while Kristi and Pamela rotated their breasts on the windows and even added some flavor using their fingers on their nipples. The effect was nothing short of cataclysmic as the men whooped and hollered for them to "work it," "ooh-la-la" and "yeah, baby."

Meanwhile, Violet heard the signal. She opened the H-1 dayroom door a crack, peering in just enough to see the backsides of the cheering cadets. Above their heads, she could see one set of buttocks and two pairs of breasts, like bookends, pushed against the windows. Jan's face was not visible and she could only see Kristi and Pamela's ski-masked heads.

She tiptoed along the wall to her left, pressed the "eject" button on the VCR player, then slowly and quietly removed the videotape. She pressed it under her sweatshirt and tiptoed back to the hallway, gently closing the door behind her.

"Now!" Kristi shouted a second time. The three friends stood, pulling their clothes back to the proper positions before fleeing along the narrow path toward the opposite end of the building. They navigated over an iron fence and down a short stairway to a set of large wooden doors leading to the basement of the adjoining building, which housed the Cadet Store and administrative offices on its upper floors. The trio ran the length of the dark hallway, illuminated only by red exit signs.

At the last one, they turned right and scurried up another flight of stairs before arriving back outside through a second set of wooden doors. Executing a left face, they trotted down a small ramp onto the sidewalk of Thayer Road, where they slowed to a casual walk, giggling all the way back to New South.

TWENTY-FOUR

"My decision to register women confirms what is already obvious throughout our society—that women are now providing all types of skills in every profession. The military should be no exception."
(President Jimmy Carter)

February 5, 1983
2030 hours

Jan and Rivers went on their first official date the following Saturday night. Like most yearlings, Jan wasn't allowed to leave Post, which meant their romantic dinner out consisted of pizza and beer, in uniform, at Ike Hall. Still, Jan knew that a firstie would not normally stay on Post over the weekend.

Obviously, he likes me.

She asked him if he had heard anything about H-1's "missing" videotape. Thankfully, he seemed unaware of the covert operation. Then she asked what he thought about Joey Lishiski. Rivers wasn't the type to speak badly about anyone, but he said he didn't care much for "Mr. Lishiski."

Two for two.

"Okay, one more question." She figured he would earn the

right to ask her a few questions after this one. "What have you heard about Kristi and me?"

Rivers put his pizza slice down. "Well, of course, we've all heard the whole story—about how you followed Cadet—"

"Wait!" She couldn't let him continue. "We didn't *follow* him. We were exploring, when we *came upon* him."

"Okay, you guys 'came upon him.'" His braces gleamed through his smile. "Then you guys defended yourselves, which is how—how—well, you know."

"Is that all?"

"That's all I've ever heard."

"Nothing else?"

"Well, of course, I heard you also had been in an Honor Board last year," he admitted.

"And?"

"And you were absolved."

"That's it?"

"That's all I've heard."

She decided she could believe him. "Okay, your turn."

He proceeded to ask about the three "F's"—her family, her friends and what she does for fun. She kept thinking how enjoyable it was to talk about "normal" stuff.

Finally, a conversation with another cadet—a male one, no less—that doesn't involve studying, the Honor Code or sex.

Well, at least right then it didn't.

They ended date night in Washington Hall. Jan's aversion to the basement levels meant they took the elevator to the top floor. The sixth floor housed a large, loud room called "the computer room." Approximately fifty computers, almost the size of their footlockers, were lined up on tables, in the center of the room like a formation. Even larger printers sat on tables around the perimeter of the room. On the floor beneath every printer, a bulky roll of paper fed into a large rotating drum. The drum's "teeth" grasped the holes on each side and turned the paper while a needle scrolled back and forth, printing.

The computers, and especially the printers, made it nearly impossible to hear. Communicating in the computer room required screaming or sign language. Jan once saw two cadets "speaking" using infantry signals.

"I'm ready, are you ready?" One cadet waved his hand back and forth above his head.

"Freeze." The other cadet signaled by making a fist at eye level.

"Double time." The first one seemed to shout by raising and lowering his fist in the air.

"Team leader forward, to rally point." The other signaled by tapping his forehead twice, then making small circles above his head and pointing to the computer room door.

"Move out." His friend signaled back by raising his arm in the air and letting it fall forward.

"Understood." A thumbs-up was the final gesture.

Normally, Jan made a point of staying as far away from the computer room as possible. The loud racket reverberated in her brain many hours later and often gave her headaches. But all that noise on the sixth floor of Washington Hall also had its advantages.

Jan and Rivers slipped past the doors of the computer room, sneaking down a short, perpendicular hallway before stealthily entering a storage room. Stacks of cardboard boxes lined the back wall; mops, brooms and brushes hung on the left wall. Stacked in neat piles against the right wall were folded carpet remnants and drop cloths.

That's where they fell.

Normally, January and February at West Point passed with agonizing slowness, but the gray days of winter whizzed by for the young couple. Rivers gave up weekends away from West Point and Jan began having fun for the first time in her college career. Every free hour she met Rivers in her room, in his room, in the library's mezzanine floors, in Thayer and Mahan classrooms after hours, and of course, in the infamous storage room at the top of Washington Hall.

She enjoyed the sex, although not nearly as much as Rivers. Jan still couldn't figure out what all the hype was about. Yeah, it felt good to be touched and kissed all over, but where was this "orgasm" thing that Kristi and Esther said was spectacular? Jan decided she was going to bug Esther about that book after all.

On the last Friday in February, *The New York Times* article about ex-cadet Wan arrived at everyone's door. Jan read it out loud to Leslie and Esther.

What's Happening to Women at West Point?
(Part 2)
By Steve Calibrio, staff writer

Last month, my article titled "What's Happening to Women at West Point" highlighted the staggering number of women who have recently left USMA and some of the reasons why they have resigned. I had expected to hear from many, like me, who are outraged at this hidden travesty. Yet I was taken aback by the visceral response from those who feel that women should never have been allowed to become cadets. I was shocked and disappointed to hear from many who actually believe that "females got what they deserved" when they entered the gates of West Point.

I don't even know what to say to that. Except that there's a whole lot of ignorance out there. And I'm not going to beat the dead horse of why women should be allowed to attend our nation's service academies. That battle has already been fought and won. I'm sorry for those sore losers who cannot accept the reality that our world has changed for the better—allowing opportunities for women that were once only available for men.

For those who can't seem to accept social progress, I suggest you pack up and emigrate to Afghanistan, the Congo, or Nepal—where women are valued a little lower than sheep and goats. Those places might be just where you belong.

In the meantime, I'm going to continue to write about what's happening to women at West Point.

Recently, one woman's story came to my attention that highlights the need to deal with the issues facing these brave young women. This woman has agreed to share her story here in the hopes that it might help all women in uniform.

Her father is a 1958 graduate and she grew up hearing stories of his days at West Point. Through the years she met many of his classmates, now lifelong friends. Her mother also became close to many of the other wives. Neither parent ever imagined their only daughter could or would become a cadet.

She followed every story about the first women who entered West Point in the summer of 1976. She was only fourteen and still had time to prepare.

And prepare, she did. She studied diligently, she ran and was elected for student government, she joined several service clubs, and she played every sport her school offered for girls—softball, basketball and lacrosse. She knew what it would take to get into West Point and she made sure she had covered all the bases. She wanted to have what her dad had—a top-notch education at the historic, preeminent military academy—making lifelong friends and jump-starting a successful military career.

Her diligence paid off and she entered West Point in the summer of 1980, following the graduation of the first class with women. She was a vibrant, eager young woman, excited to be following in her father's footsteps.

Plebe year was tough, as it is designed to be. Yet she endured and did well, having the benefit of her father's advice. She started yearling year at Camp Buckner where she continued to thrive and receive high praise from her leaders and peers. She entered the academic year in the Fourth Regiment where she met her first boyfriend—a handsome young man in her company.

They dated for a few months, and as most college students are known to do, they began having sex.

Now, before you make judgments about cadets having sex, think back to what you were doing in college. Were you having sex? I bet you were. Did you have a girlfriend or a boyfriend? Well, cadets do too. And yes, they have sex.

This young woman was responsible. Her mother had talked to her about birth control and she had prepared for her sexual life. She would not get pregnant.

And she did not get pregnant. Instead, she was raped.

She dated her handsome boyfriend for all of sophomore year and then into junior year. They argued occasionally over silly things and made up quickly. But one night, they had a big fight. It was one of those serious, gut-wrenching, breakup fights. They both agreed not to see each other again. That was that, she thought.

Did you know that there are no locks on cadet room doors?

Later that night, after Taps, she fell asleep alone in her room while her roommate was away at a swim meet. Someone snuck into her room and into her bed. She woke up as he was pulling down her underwear.

She screamed. Or she thought she screamed. Therapists have since told her that she probably felt like she was screaming, but in fact, may not have made any noise. It would have been a normal reaction to her intense fear.

She continued screaming and fighting him, but he was able to hold her down. At first, she didn't realize who was on top of her. But then he spoke. He said something she will never forget.

"I can still get this from you anytime I want."

It was his voice. She knew, without any doubt, that her ex-boyfriend—the son of one of the top military officers at West Point (she refused to be more specific for fears of continued repercussions) had just raped her.

After the initial shock and fear wore off, she made her way to the women's latrine. All alone and crying uncontrollably, she showered in the middle of the night. She didn't even think about preserving evidence. She couldn't think about anything other than the fact that the boy she once loved had just horribly and irrevocably violated her.

She also knew she couldn't spend the rest of her cadet life wondering if he would come back for more. She knew she would never look at him without seeing what he did over and over again.

She showered for over two hours, somehow finding the resolve to fight back.

The next morning, she reported to her TAC—the company officer in charge of cadets. She told him what happened. To his credit, the TAC believed her. He was willing to report it up the chain of command. But he warned her that she would have to file formal charges accusing a high-ranking officer's son of a heinous crime and there would be many who would not believe her.

She was willing to take those risks. She could not let the young man get away with his crime.

So she did what needed to be done. She filed charges with the MPs, she spoke to several "investigating officers" and she gave her testimony at a "hearing." Then she waited for her ex-boyfriend's arrest, or, at the very least, his expulsion.

But nothing happened to the young man. In fact, he seemed more popular than ever, while she was practically silenced by her company mates. Even women cadets began to distance themselves from her. Except for a few brave friends, everyone in the battalion gave her the cold shoulder.

Very shortly after that, her company Honor representative paid her a visit. He informed her that she was being investigated for an Honor violation. The findings of the "criminal investigation," she was told then, determined that she and her boyfriend merely had consensual sex—something they had done before in her room—and that her accusations were an attempt to discredit the young man after they had broken up.

She stared, open-mouthed, at the firstie who delivered this news. How did they determine it was consensual, she asked? He told her the young man admitted to having sex with her and everyone knew they were a couple.

There it was. She had been ambushed. Again. She knew how the Honor Trial would go. These things rarely go well for anyone, never mind for a woman who accuses a "prince" of rape. She knew she had been beaten.

She packed her bags and went home the next day.

This, dear readers, is why we must continue to find out and correct what's happening to women at West Point.

TWENTY-FIVE

ODIN, n. A Norwegian god to whom cadets appeal for rain before parades, inspection, etc.
(Cadet Slang, Bugle Notes, 81, p.291)

March 10, 1983
1545 Hours

Spring arrived at USMA, ushering in a new parade season. Once again, the Corps of Cadets spent every Tuesday and Thursday afternoon marching back and forth on the Plain.

Jan and Esther donned the white belts and bayonet over their class uniform and gray jacket, grabbed their M-14's, stored on a rack by the sink cabinet, and headed outside for drill formation.

Company G-1 formed up in New South Area along with companies H-1 and I-1. The battalion commander shouted, "BA-TTAL-ION," each company commander yelled, "COM-PANY," then each platoon leader echoed, "PLA-TOON." The process began again with a specific order: "Forward march!"

They marched down the ramp to Central Area, lining up behind the rest of First Regiment. As one, the four regiments emerged through the four sally ports of Washington Hall for the usual afternoon drill. Once in position on the field, they stood at attention, awaiting the order to "present arms." They did this several times before forward marching again in a long column, by regiments, by battalions, by companies, by platoons, until the entire Corps of Cadets passed in front of the dignitaries' platform.

Approaching this spot, each company commander yelled, "Present arms!" In unison, cadets brought the nine-and-a-half pound M-14s from resting on their right shoulders to a vertical position in front of their bodies, bayonet tip lined up with the top of their eyebrows. While in this saluting position, the commanders gave another order: "Eyes, right!" The company snapped their heads to the right simultaneously. They marched from thirty to fifty paces in this position, depending on the size of the viewing party.

A downpour on Friday night gave hope to the cadets that the first parade of the season might be cancelled. However, their prayers to Odin went unanswered as the weather cleared and the sun came out just in time for Saturday's festivities.

After classes, Company G-1 formed up in full dress gray over gray. Every cadet wore white criss-crossed belts with polished brass plates in the center of every breast, along with white gloves and the funny plastic hat with plume sticking out the top like a rude gesture. The four regiments proceeded to march onto the Plain as practiced.

The grass, still wet from the rain, elicited whispers of "step carefully" and "watch your step" from the upperclassmen to the less experienced plebes. Company G-1 marched uneventfully onto the Plain and took its spot in the long gray line of cadets. They stood at attention, presented arms, stood at ease, then at attention and presented arms again, before beginning to make the wide arc in front of the dignitaries box.

At the right spot, John Heggenbach ordered, "Present arms." Everyone in G-1 moved the M-14s from their right shoulders to front vertical position, as they had practiced.

"Eyes, right!"

All of G-1 snapped their heads to the right, paying respect to the guests of honor.

That's when all hell broke loose in First Platoon.

Somewhere in the front-middle of the platoon, a cadet lost his footing on the wet grass and slipped to the left. He fell onto the cadet next to him and that cadet slipped backward, falling completely on the ground. The cadet behind that one also went down, along with the two on either side of him. Jan, marching in the back, far left, with her eyes right, could see the commotion.

Quiet grumbles of "watch out," "get up," "move over," "idiot," and "moron" were audible among First Platoon. Another two or three cadets almost tripped over each other trying to move around the fallen soldiers, who were now jumping back up and trying to realign themselves in the formation. The rest of the platoon continued marching as if this was all very normal.

Jan noticed that a hole had opened up to her right. Keeping in step, she marched to that spot, opening a spot on the outside left, which was quickly filled by one of the disoriented cadets. Others followed suit. All of this shifting to accommodate the "fallen" cadets on the left flank was done with "eyes right" and in "present arms" mode. By the time the platoon rounded the corner turning away from the viewing stand, First Platoon was back in formation, just a little scrambled around.

Once back in New South Area, John Heggenbach dismissed the company, never realizing what had happened right behind him. First Platoon leader Guy Hernandez turned around and said, "What the hell happened out there?"

"Cadet Jones fell over onto Cadet Davis, who fell over onto Cadet McGuire and Cadet Gonsalez," someone shouted.

Esther was among the fallen? Jan said a silent prayer for

her. A fallen cadet was bad; a fallen *female* cadet could be traumatizing.

Guy Hernandez looked at Cadet Jones, a plebe, and said, "What happened, Jones?"

"Sir, I slipped."

"You slipped?"

"Yes, sir."

"Do you know, Jones, that in the history of West Point, no one has ever accomplished what you did today?" Hernandez asked with dead seriousness while most of the platoon began chuckling. "Because of you, Jones, First Platoon, Company G-1, will go down in history as the only platoon to march in a fuster cluck!"

"Yes, sir!" Jones seemed a little proud of his part.

"Thanks, Jones. Thanks for that distinction."

"Any time, sir!"

"No, Jones! Once is enough!"

Jan and Esther walked back to their room and began dismantling their "P-rade" uniform. They were halfway finished when someone knocked on their door.

"C'm in," Jan said.

Guy Hernandez and John Heggenbach, still in full Parade uniform, stood in the hallway.

"I heard about what happened," John said.

There were half a dozen others who fell over—why's he gotta get on Esther about it?

"She wasn't the only one to fall, John," Jan said defensively.

"I didn't say she was," he replied.

"Yeah, well, if you're gonna get on her case for it then you better go see all the others, too." Jan was not about to let him single out her roommate.

"Geez, Jan," Guy said, "calm down."

She reddened, but didn't let up. "You joked with Jones about it, but now you're all business when it comes to the one female..."

"Jan," John clamored.

"What?"

Esther spoke up. "Look, I feel bad enough about it..."

"Will you both just shut up?" Guy shouted.

Jan and Esther stood silent, stunned, waiting to be reprimanded.

"What I *heard*," John looked at Jan, "was how you side-stepped in the middle of the fiasco while marching, with eyes right, to make room on the outside flank for our fallen soldiers."

Huh? You mean you're not here to criticize us?

The company commander continued, "And I wanted to commend you for your quick thinking."

"Uh..." She quickly rewired her brain to accept that he wasn't looking to pick a fight. "I...I just saw an opening next to me and moved into it."

"Yes, Jan. And it did not go unnoticed. Well done."

"Uh, thanks."

John and Guy turned toward their rooms while Jan closed the door softly.

"I guess we shouldn't assume they're always out to get us," Esther said.

"Yeah, suppose so," Jan replied.

Esther opened her desk drawer and pulled out a paperback book. "Here's that book I told you about." She handed it to her roommate.

Jan read the title: *Reaching Orgasm—A Woman's Guide to Sexual Climax.* "Oh my God, Esther, where the hell am I gonna read this?" She began leafing through the pages.

It has drawings, for cryin'-out-loud! Graphic pictures of down there!

Never having seen pornography, Jan was sure this book could be considered in that category. "Shit, where the hell am I even gonna keep it?"

Esther read her thoughts. "It's not pornography, Jan."

"Uh, okay, but still...I can't be caught alive with this. Or I'll be dead."

"Just read it when you're alone and store it in your footlocker." Esther didn't seem to feel the same level of anxiety. "Of course, you'll need time to practice."

Oh, Jaysus.

Jan kept it hidden in her footlocker and pulled it out occasionally after Taps for light reading by flashlight under her Gray Girl. She never found an opportunity to "practice."

Halfway through the book, Jan began worrying about the hiding spot. Footlockers were sometimes inspected during SAMI. She thought about keeping it in the laundry bag, but every so often, those were also pulled out and dumped of their contents. She felt certain that if the book were to be discovered in her possession, she would never be able to live it down.

She formulated a plan. Taking the paper cover off another book, she placed it over *Reaching Orgasm.* The coverless book, *To Kill a Mockingbird*, went into her footlocker. The newly-concealed book went on her bookshelf, arranged in height order, with all the other books.

Ingenious. Hidden in plain sight.

TWENTY-SIX

"If we weren't all crazy we would go insane."
(Jimmy Buffet)

March 11, 1983
2300 Hours

A weekend pass allowed the young lovers to escape to New York City in Rivers' blue 1968 Mustang. The first night, they parked on a busy street, leaving the car locked while they went to a new movie called *The Return of Martin Guerre.* Jan thoroughly enjoyed the film, especially since it was her first real date—as in not in uniform, not in the back seat of a car and not in a storage room—date.

After the movie they returned to the Mustang to discover that Rivers' stereo, CB radio, police scanner and guitar were all gone. Yet the car remained locked.

"That was kind of them," Jan groused.

Rivers didn't seem to mind the loss of his property as much. "Well, I guess it's a small price to pay," he said.

"How can you say that? They just stole several thousand dollars of your stuff."

"Yeah, I'm gonna need a whole lot of lovin' to make up for

it," he said, smiling through his braces.

They spent the rest of the weekend eating out, sleeping in and boinking their brains out.

These were her USMA "salad days," she would later realize. She had no idea they would be the last, great days of her cadet life.

She returned to her room Sunday evening to find Rick Davidson sitting at her desk.

"Oh, hey." She said, trying to sound neutral.

"Hey, Jan." He stood up. "I wanted to be the first to tell you that Captain Hasuko has been removed as coach."

"What?"

"He's been replaced already, some major from Fourth Reg."

"Why?" Jan's voice cracked.

"Don't know...our coach told us at practice yesterday."

Leslie, sitting on her bed, said, "We also heard a few professors have been 're-assigned,'" she said, using her fingers as quotation marks. "Major Behar was one of them."

"When?" Jan remained standing in the same spot. "What the hell is going on?"

"My guess is it has to do with that last article in *The New York Times*," Leslie said.

"I agree," Rick said. "Someone had to have shared something with Calibrio."

"Cadet Wan herself did," Jan argued.

"Yeah, but someone had to have told him about her and how to contact her," Rick said.

"The point is," Leslie added, "they all got sacked for trying to help."

"Shit, I've got to call Drew." She ran from the room and down the hall to the pay phone booth.

The week went by in a haze as Jan tried to accept her new Arabic professor and coach. Neither substitute seemed as good or as competent as the original ones. Certainly, she could not confide in either of them. The replacements had taken over Hasuko's and Behar's offices and no one seemed to know where the predecessors had been relocated. Jan felt sure they were still on Post, but where?

Her only consolation was that Drew might be able to contact them and find out what happened and why. Jan was fairly certain they were sacked for the article about Cadet Wan. That meant that Kristi, Pamela and Jan would also be targeted. She decided the best course of action was to lay low and hopefully all would blow over before the powers-that-be found them out.

The following Saturday, Guy Hernandez, John Heggenbach, Myrna Watkins and Captain Landau, entered their room for SAMI. Jan knew this meant trouble. Normally, only squad leaders and platoon leaders conducted the Saturday AM Inspection.

And so it starts…

"Good morning, ladies," the TAC said.

"Good morning, sir," the three roommates replied in unison.

First, Landau opened their laundry bins. He pulled out Leslie's green laundry bag and began feeling the outside. He did the same with Esther's. With Jan's bag, he dumped the contents into the sink. A few t-shirts, a couple pairs of underwear and a bra came tumbling out. He threw the bag on top of the items before moving to their closets.

Landau leaned all the way into each closet, running his hand along the back of the shelves. He stood upright again. "Dusty closets," he said while brushing his hands together. Guy Hernandez noted the infraction on a clipboard.

Jan smirked slightly at John Heggenbach. His eyes stared

back at her with no expression.

Uh-oh.

The TAC continued inspecting, noticing that the beds were not tight enough to bounce a quarter. Another jot went on the clipboard by Guy.

"Open your footlockers, ladies," Captain Landau ordered.

Jan, Esther and Leslie got out their keys and squatted down in front of their trunks. Each cadet opened the black boxes and pulled out the removable top shelves.

Leslie had candy bars, Esther had several bags of chips and Jan had *To Kill a Mockingbird.*

"Contraband," Landau remarked, throwing the candy bars and chips onto their floor. Guy noted it on the clipboard.

"Miss Wishart, I see you have a copy of my favorite book," Landau said while holding up the real one.

"Yes, sir," she said, hoping he wouldn't notice the other "copy" on her bookshelf.

Landau dropped the book back in her footlocker, stood erect and walked to the desk area. He focused on Leslie's first, running his hand along her bookshelves for dust. Not finding any, he turned to Esther's desk. He picked up the one picture frame cadets were authorized to have on their desks. It was a photo of Esther and Adam Nutter, her boyfriend.

"You dating Cadet Nutter, Miss Gonsalez?" Landau asked.

"Yes, sir," she said.

"That's fine. As long as you keep your business off Post, that is."

"Yes, sir," she replied.

Then Landau turned to Jan's desk area. Jan's one picture was of her with two high school friends. "What about you, Miss Wishart? Anyone special?"

Dammit, why's he asking me this shit? She could not possibly lie, even though she didn't want everyone knowing her business.

"Yes, sir."

"Really? Who's the lucky guy?"

"Sir, he's not in our company." She hoped that would suffice.

"But he's a cadet, right?" Landau asked.

"Yes, sir."

"Well, then, do tell."

What an asshole. "Cadet Preston, sir."

"Ah, yes, in H-1, right?"

"Yes, sir."

Landau swiped her bookshelves for dust. Then he examined her books, lined from tallest to shortest, in accordance with the regulations. "Oh, I see you have two copies of *To Kill a Mockingbird*," Landau exclaimed while pulling it off her shelf.

Oh shit!

"I love this book too, it was my favorite as a kid." Jan froze in horror and prayed he wouldn't open it up.

Please put it back! Put it back, please!

"Have you ever read this, John?" Landau asked while holding the book out toward the CO.

"No, sir. I've only seen the movie," John replied.

"Here," he tossed the book to Heggenbach, "I'm sure Miss Wishart won't mind if you borrow one of her copies."

Oh God, no!

To Jan's terror, John began thumbing through the book. Landau continued to walk around the room looking for dust, dirt, and things out of place. But Jan remained fixed on her company commander—her first-time lover—holding her pornographic book in his hands. This would be the end of her life as she knew it. The graphic drawings alone would seal her fate.

He will ruin me. They will all come looking for "favors" for the rest of my cadet life.

Jan held her breath in anticipation of John Heggenbach's reaction to what he had to know by now was not the TAC's childhood classic. Blood rushed to her face, her fingers began to tingle. John sifted through the book some more, shifting his weight from one foot to the other.

This little "gift" from Esther will forever mark me as the G-1 whore. I will always be known as the one with "the dirty little book."

In a fog, Jan heard the TAC ask Leslie a question. She heard Leslie say something. Jan's heart seemed to stop beating as, trance-like, she waited for the judgment that would seal her fate.

John Heggenbach snapped the book shut and looked at Jan with an expression she could not read. The inspection was over. The TAC walked out their door, followed by Guy, clipboard in hand, and Myrna. John trailed, still holding her pornography, closing the door behind him.

"Well, that wasn't too bad," Leslie said.

Jan, staring at the back of the door, cried out, "He's got the book, Esther!"

"What? You mean the book I gave you?"

"Yes! The very one! I put the fake cover on it to hide it on my bookshelf. That's why I have *To Kill a Mockingbird* in my footlocker."

"Jan, what the hell were you thinking?" Esther asked.

Leslie, not understanding the gravity of the situation asked, "What's the book—a communist manifesto, how to assassinate a president, how to cheat without getting caught?"

Jan slumped her shoulders. "Much worse."

Esther answered for her. "It's a book about how to achieve orgasms."

"Holy SHIT," Leslie giggled.

"IT'S NOT FUNNY, WRIGHT!"

Three times, Jan went to Heggenbach's room to ask for her book back. Three times, she chickened out. Even though Kristi and Pamela agreed to help her "secure" it from the enemy's hands, Jan felt she should not have to take back her own book. She simply wanted him to return it.

Like two adults…there's nothing to hide or to be ashamed of.

A couple weeks passed without incident and Jan began to think John Heggenbach might actually be reading the book for his own education.

Perhaps he'll return it after he's gleaned all he can about the female erotic zones.

TWENTY-SEVEN

"Unlike the regiments of the Army, cadet companies have no collective battle heritage, however, the contributions of former cadets to the leadership of American soldiers in battle in all this country's wars is unrivaled by any other institution in the world. This theme of past accomplishments and potential for future contributions should form the unifying theme of a cadet dining in."

(Guide to Military Dining-In, Cadet Hostess Office)

March 19, 1983
1830 hours

"Ladies and gentlemen, I propose a toast to the Commander-in-Chief, The President of the United States," The battalion commander shouted while lifting his wine glass from his place at the head table.

The battalion-wide Dining-In, a formal dinner held in the spring every year, was meant to instill camaraderie and cohesion among the companies. Women wore the "dress mess" uniform—a long black skirt, a short-sleeved white blouse with pearl buttons and a black tab collar, a black cummerbund and a waist-cut white coat with gold epaulets. Black low-heeled pumps closed out the ensemble. It was the closest they ever came to looking sexy in uniform, yet it covered every square inch of their skin, except their face. The male cadets wore the full dress gray coat over white trousers.

"To the president," Companies G, H and I, still standing, responded in unison while raising their glasses.

The Black, Gray and Gold Room in Washington Hall held thirty tables, ten for each company, surrounded by ten cadets each. Jan took a sip of wine while standing at one of the G-1 tables toward the back of the room. She spotted Kristi, Pamela and Violet together in the H-1 section. Rivers sipped his wine at a nearby table with his classmates.

"Ladies and gentlemen, I propose a toast to the United States Army," John Heggenbach announced from the head table.

"To the Army!" Everyone lifted their glasses again and took another sip of wine.

"Ladies and gentlemen, I propose a toast to the United States Military Academy," H Company commander bellowed.

"To the Academy!" Another lift and sip.

"Ladies and gentlemen, I propose a toast to the Corps of Cadets." It was the I Company commander's turn.

"To the Corps!"

Then the battalion XO announced, "Gentlemen, please seat your ladies."

Jan never knew what to expect at this point. Was she a lady? If so, whose lady? Would anyone pull out her chair?

She looked toward the H-1 section and saw male cadets seating all three of her friends. She noticed Rivers pulling out the chair for a female classmate at his table.

Then she looked to her table. No one was moving. Every one of her classmates remained standing behind his chair.

Nope. I'm no one's lady.

"Jan," someone whispered in her right ear, almost causing her to drop her glass. "If you would be so kind as to step aside," Rick said nodding toward her chair.

"Oh," she said, moving slightly to her left.

He pulled out her chair and motioned for her to sit down, saying, "Please be seated, ma'am."

"Uh...thanks," she managed after a pause.

"Gentlemen, I propose a toast...to the ladies."

"To the ladies!" the standing male cadets toasted the now seated female cadets.

Jan raised her glass as well. "To the gentlemen," she said softly while looking up at Rick.

"Gentlemen, please be seated," came the final announcement.

The mess hall staff brought out huge covered platters and set them down on each table. The waiters removed the large silver lids to expose Chicken Kiev and baked potatoes. A third platter on every table revealed a mound of steaming broccoli. The feasting began.

Two bottles of wine—one red and one white—had been appointed at each table. Jan poured herself the red wine knowing that most cadets preferred white. It was her lucky night, as half the table was not drinking at all. Jan never understood why some cadets refused perfectly good free wine. Additionally, she knew that she, Kristi, Pamela and a few good men would scrounge around afterwards making sure all the wine had been consumed.

Someone has to do it.

She glanced toward Rivers' table and could tell he was enjoying the festivities. It was their first Dining-In together, sort–of, and he caught her eye. He smiled at her. Then, she realized with sadness, it was also their last. His next Dining-In would be with his unit somewhere in the Army. She would enjoy two more as a cadet, if she lasted that long.

The guys at Jan's table talked, laughed and joked. She poured herself more wine and kept smiling at nothing in particular, figuring it was better to smile than to frown. It seemed to her they did not want to include her in their conversation, which caused her to feel somewhat invisible. Sipping her wine, she decided she liked being ignored and she smiled at the thought.

The wait staff brought the final large platter for each table, along with a pot of coffee. When the lid was removed, they discovered a vast array of petit fours. There were at least forty on the platter, giving each cadet about four each. But when the platter made its way around the table, arriving to Jan last, only one petit four remained.

"I'll stick with wine for dessert," she announced as she placed the huge platter and its single occupant down. Lifting the red wine bottle, she drained the last of its contents into her glass.

"Ladies and gentlemen," the battalion first sergeant announced, "the plebes of First Battalion will now present a short skit for tonight's entertainment. Please direct your attention to the back of the room."

Jan turned around in her chair, noticing a small open space behind the rows of tables. Everyone began adjusting their chairs to view the "stage." Jan's seat was now in the front row.

Two cadets walked toward each other, one holding up a videotape. "Hey, we just got a new movie—you wanna watch with us?"

"Sure, what's it about?" asked the other.

"Um..." The cadet holding the videotape looked left and right. "It's kind of classified...you'll just have to wait and see."

"Oh, geez, not another spy movie..." Chuckling punctuated the room.

"But it's not your *average* spy movie..." The chuckling continued.

"Well, is it more like a western, a mystery, a thriller, a comedy?"

"I think it could be considered a romance." More laughter.

"I don't want to watch a stupid romance."

"Okay, suit yourself." And the plebe with the videotape walked off.

Jan kept a smile plastered on her face, despite the heat rising in her neck.

The remaining cadet started pacing, thinking out loud, "There's never anything interesting going on around here...it's always so boring, same old thing every day."

A couple of male plebes walked into view wearing female cadet skirts and wigs. They held open a *New York Times* newspaper, reading as they walked. The pacing plebe asked them what they were reading.

"Oh, nothing important," one wigged plebe said in a high-pitched voice. The laughter started again.

"Are you reading the article about the female cadets?" asked his "classmate."

"Why, whatever do you mean?" the other "female" replied, shocked. Jan could hear snickering behind her.

"You mean you don't know anything about it?" the first cadet asked indignantly.

"We can neither confirm nor deny anything," the wigged plebes said before storming off stage.

Jan didn't dare look around. She held the same smile, wondering if anyone could see through it.

The original cadet continued to pace, thinking out loud again. "See what I mean...nothing exciting ever happens..."

The next vignette depicted a marching scene where several cadets fell and tripped over each other. It generated the loudest and most raucous laughter, which felt somewhat comforting to Jan.

Several more scenes followed portraying a cadet's hometown girlfriend confronting him as he walked with his cadet girlfriend; a dumpster diving incident involving three inebriated cadets; and a firstie mission to hire "waitresses" at the O'Club.

Jan finally released her smile and her breath when the entertainment ended and everyone turned their chairs back to face the front of the room. She knew it could have been much worse and felt relieved and thankful that the role playing didn't go any further than it did.

Still.

She glanced at Kristi and Pamela, both of whom nodded in return. She was sure they had been feeling the same thing. She looked toward Rivers. He smiled at her. She couldn't tell if it was an "it's okay" smile or an "I'm embarrassed" smile. Jan felt certain he received lots of ribbing for dating her and tonight's entertainment only added to her feeling that she was weighing him down. She felt like his ball and chain.

Jan stood and picked up the white wine bottle. "Anyone for a refill?" she asked everyone and no one all at once. Then she poured a few glasses for those who nodded in assent, before refilling her own. This was drink number four.

It's going to be a great night.

"C'mon, Pamela, get in!" Jan whispered loudly as the trio squeezed into the small elevator. All year, Pamela had been asking Jan and Kristi to show her the "scene of the crime." And all year, both Jan and Kristi had been unwilling to revisit and re-enact the devastating events. But after the battalion Dining-In and six or eight glasses of wine, they were sufficiently drunk enough to face those demons once again.

The elevator was not meant for three, but they managed to squeeze in and close the metal door, which activated the downward movement. Just like last year, no buttons were pushed. The elevator just descended once the doors closed.

Eerie!

The doors automatically opened when they reached the small office. It looked exactly as they remembered it. A small desk, a couch and a door on the left, which led to a hallway and a small room—the place where they witnessed something they both tried to forget. The other door in the hallway had been their only escape route—a stairway, leading up to the kitchen and the mess hall, where Kristi had fought a battle for her life.

Jan shuddered at the memory. If she hadn't been drunk, she knew she would never have made this journey to the "underworld" again. Pamela was fascinated. "So this is where you heard something?"

"Yeah," Kristi said, "we thought they were laughing at first."

They walked down the hallway to the small room on the left and opened the door. Paint cans were still lined up near the entrance but the table was gone. The room looked like a graveyard, with broken chairs stacked and strewn, seemingly waiting for either repair or burial.

"Where old chairs go to die," Jan mumbled.

They turned to go.

"Wait, what's this?" Kristi bent down and picked up something shiny and small. She brought it out to the hallway so they could see it better. It was Airborne Wings. Jan and Kristi exchanged glances, knowing which dress gray coat this silver pin had fallen from.

"I think we've seen enough, don't you?" Jan asked. "This is putting a damper on the evening's festivities."

"Yeah, I guess so, I just wanted to see where everything happened…" Pamela sounded apologetic.

"Okay, well, now you've seen it. Let's go." Jan didn't want to linger any longer.

At a slower pace, they took the same route as last year, up the stairs, through a kitchen and out into the darkened mess hall.

"Hey, guys, I just want to go up to the poop deck, I've never been up there," Pamela said.

"There's nothing up there," Jan replied.

"I want to see the view." Pamela entered the stairwell leading to the Poop deck while Jan and Kristi waited below.

"I don't have a need to go up there, do you?" Jan asked her old roommate.

"No, none at all," Kristi said.

They watched at the base of the massive stone balcony as Pamela looked down from above. "Hey, you guys should see this."

"See what?" they both asked from below.

"The view, it's so cool. You probably didn't get to see it when you were here..."

"No, I think we were a little preoccupied," Jan mumbled.

"C'mon up, it's quite something."

"No thanks." Jan wasn't about to go up there if she didn't have to.

"I'll take a look-see," Kristi said. "I might as well relive the whole event since I'm here." She took off to climb the steps to where Pamela was perched.

I don't know what the big deal is...

Jan paced below the poop deck, waiting for her friends to come back down. She figured it wouldn't be more than a couple minutes. But after what seemed like five minutes, Jan called up to them, "Hey, when are you guys coming down?"

No answer.

"Hey, Pamela, Kristi, c'mon down!"

No answer.

"Guys, what are you doing up there?"

No answer.

Shit.

"Quit messing around, I mean it!"

Nothing.

"This isn't funny!"

Nada.

Dammit.

"Okay, fine. Have it your way." Jan stormed up the steps to the poop deck.

She didn't feel afraid until she reached the top and looked across the length of the platform to the opposite stairwell leading back down. With no sign of Pamela or Kristi, Jan tiptoed slowly into the space between the stairways. "Guys, you up here?"

Still no answer.

Jan's skin began to tingle. She could feel her muscles tightening. Everything went on high alert.

After only two steps, she noticed the dark stain in the middle of the cement floor. They hadn't been able to get rid of it completely. It had been sealed forever into the stone balcony. Immortalized.

Don't look at it, she told herself, but she did anyway. Something about the shape of the bloodstain was mesmerizing. *What is it? An animal of some kind, I think...*

The more she stared at it, the more she felt drawn to it...like it held some deep secret. If only she could identify the shape of the bloodstain, then she could understand all of life. That's what her alcohol-addled mind told her, anyway.

Enough of this! I have to find Pamela and Kristi. She bent down, crept to the right side and placed her hand on the stone balustrade while ducking below the level of the top. This way, she didn't have to look over the edge of the three-story tower. Halfway along the deck, her hand skimmed over something on the railing.

Jan stopped. She felt it again.

A plaque?

She fingered the raised lettering inside a rectangular box. *I don't remember this being here last year.* She stood up, vowing not to look over the edge.

The moonlight shining in the stained glass window at the front of Washington Hall coupled with the tinted red light of the exit signs were just enough light for her to read the inscription.

Ut sementem feceris ita metes.

She heard giggling from below. "Ha, ha! We knew there would be only one way to get you up there!" Kristi shouted up to her from the mess hall floor.

"Assholes!" Jan shouted, breaking her vow by looking down at them. "Hey, did you see this?"

"See what?" Pamela asked.

"Get up here, assholes, and I'll show you."

The three friends gathered around the inscription and memorized the Latin words, which took much longer than it should have. They had no idea what it meant, but they knew exactly who would.

The trio gathered around Rick's desk as he looked through his book of Latin phrases. Jan hoped his actions at the Dining-In and his help finding the translation meant that he had forgiven her. But his body language seemed to suggest something else. He leaned away from her as he read. *"Ut sementem feceris ita metes* means: *As you sow, so shall you reap."*

They stood silently for a long moment pondering the phrase's significance.

"What the hell is that supposed to mean?" Pamela asked.

Kristi said, "It's pretty obvious, isn't it?"

"Yeah, but who would have gone to the trouble of having a plaque made?" Jan asked incredulously. "And who would have authorized it?"

"Maybe they didn't need permission, Jan," Rick said. "It's not like anyone checks for 'unauthorized plaque usage,' especially in an inconspicuous place like the inner poop deck railing."

Pamela added, "Well, you don't need to worry about it. Most people wouldn't have a clue what it means even if they did see it."

"The problem is," Kristi said looking at Jan, "It's not meant for most people. It's only meant for us."

TWENTY-EIGHT

Q. What is Sunday night poop?
A. Six bells and all is well. Another week shot to hell. Another week in my little gray cell. Another week in which to excel. Oh, hell.
(Heritage, Bugle Notes, 81, p. 247)

March 22, 1983
1500 hours

"What the hell is this, Myrna?" Jan held up a rectangular piece of white paper as she barged into the room of her previous roommate and present squad leader.

"You know exactly what it is," Myrna retorted calmly.

"Actually, I need help with it." Jan read aloud from the 2-1, or disciplinary report, "Cadet Wishart went off limits after the battalion Dining-In—first to the basement and then to the poop deck of Washington Hall during academic hours."

"Yes, that's right," Myrna replied without affect.

"One, where did you get your information? And two, since when do you write someone up based on hearsay?"

"Are you saying you didn't go to those places after the Dining-In?"

Shit! Myrna had her by the balls, or boobs, as the saying might go.

"No, I'm not saying that."

"Then you did go off limits after the Dining-In, when you were supposed to have been on academic limits." Myrna resumed reading at her desk.

Jan stared at her former roommate. *She's has some gall writing me up for that, when she's a lesbian!*

Jan didn't care one bit about Myrna's sexual preference. But she sure as hell didn't think someone who was living a lie—and Myrna certainly had to lie about her sexual orientation—ought to point a fucking finger. It just wasn't right. *Bitch.*

"I noticed you didn't write up the other two. Surely you heard who else was with me?" Jan didn't want her friends to get in trouble, yet she didn't want to be alone in this.

"They're not in G-1. I reported it to their first sergeant. He can do what he wants."

Jan shook her head. "Okay, Myrna. I don't know what the hell I ever did to deserve this kind of treatment from you, but whatever." Jan turned and fled before she said anything worse.

The TAC awarded her a "25 and 20," meaning twenty-five demerits and twenty hours on the Area. Since leave was prohibited for cadets with twenty or more walking tours, the infraction meant Jan and Rivers' steamy plans to be together for spring leave had to be nixed.

"Well, this way you can be with friends for your last big hurrah," she said after breaking the news to Rivers.

"That's not any consolation, Jan. You know I want to be with you, right?" he asked.

Jan wasn't sure about that at all. She overheard a conversation one time whereby one cadet asked another if he had a cadet girlfriend. "No," he replied, "I date real women."

"It's the last time you will be able to go away with your friends," she said.

"But I'd rather be with you."

She would not be responsible for keeping the only firstie on Post during spring leave. And she did not want his friends riling him about being "pussy whipped."

"No, you can't stay, I won't let you do that. Just go and have fun." *Not too much fun, of course.*

By Saturday afternoon, most of the Corps had vacated the premises. The plebes were now in charge and acting every bit like the upperclassmen they would soon become. Jan stayed in her room until the first walking tour formation. Then she reported to Central Area in full dress gray over gray, under arms.

There were seven other upperclass cadets, all men, suffering the same indignity of being left behind. They lined up in a row with a handful of "beanheads," the unfortunate few who would not have the luxury of goofing off with the rest of their classmates this week.

Jan cursed Myrna Watkins. She kept wondering why Myrna seemed to have turned on her. Jan never understood why some women became worse enemies than the men. It seemed as if there were always a few "turncoats," women who would stab a fellow woman in the back, if it benefitted them. Myrna Watkins, Jan decided, was one of those types.

She began walking back and forth again. She seemed to know the rhythm of the pavement, having ingrained every divot and stain during the one hundred hours of walking she had already done. They were there again, those familiar spots, the landmarks which denoted the quarter, half and three-quarter points of every turn.

Just like old friends.

She also thought about Pamela and Kristi, probably ordering their first drink on the plane to Texas. They planned a trip to Pamela's house since Jan was supposed to have gone off with Rivers, who must have been closing in on Daytona Beach by now. He carpooled with three other firsties, which ensured they would make the sixteen-and-a-half-hour drive in fourteen hours. She prayed for their safety.

And please don't let him get drunk and sleep with some floozy. Well, okay, no way to stop him from getting drunk. Just, please, no women.

She knew Rivers was not the type to sleep around. She believed him when he said he would rather be with her than on this trip with his friends.

But still, he's a man.

She couldn't help worrying about what might happen while they were apart.

"Ma'am?" Lost in her thoughts, she almost didn't hear him.

"Ma'am?" he whispered again.

She hesitated, then continued walking. "Yes?"

"I'm Cadet Calloway, from D-4."

"And?"

"Well, ma'am, I have something that might interest you."

"Do I know you?"

"No, we've never met," he whispered. "But I've heard about you."

"Oh?"

"Yes, and I have information that will help Cadet Wan, I mean ex-cadet Wan," he whispered while keeping in step beside her.

"Why would that interest me?"

"Aren't you trying to help her?"

"I don't even know her."

"Oh." They reached the gray stones of Bradley Barracks and executed an about face simultaneously. "Sorry, I thought you were someone else, then."

"Well," she said, wanting to know, but not wanting to know, "what do you have?"

"A recording. From Cadet Mullenbehr, admitting that he raped Cadet Wan."

Jan gasped. If this guy really had a tape of the comm's son admitting his guilt, then she had to know more. "How'd you get it?"

"He's my squad leader and I saw him leaving her room that night. He had scratches and bite marks on his face. I thought maybe it was just their kind of fun until I read the article." They reached the stones of Eisenhower barracks, executed another about face and kept marching. "When he got drunk at our Dining-In, I took my recorder and went to his room." The plebe took a deep breath. "He didn't know I was taping the conversation."

"And he just admitted everything?" Jan stopped marching.

"Pretty much," he whispered

"HEY! NO TALKING OVER THERE!" The captain of the guard yelled towards them.

Jan resumed marching a step or two behind Cadet Calloway. "If you're serious, I need to get this tape...if you're interested in justice. I will get it in the right hands," she whispered from behind his back.

He slowed down until she caught up again. "Okay, meet me tonight, room 114, in the Lost Fifties, after dinner."

"I will. You better not be screwing with me, beanhead."

"I'm not, ma'am."

"Okay, I'll be there thirty minutes before Taps."

"Yes, ma'am."

Jan never knew why they were called the "Lost Fifites," other than the fact that these old barracks were the only ones that did not face onto any of the Areas: North, Central or South. And, of course, there were stories about the ghosts that supposedly inhabited them. As Jan approached the prison-like fortress of stone and iron at 2330 hours, she realized the Lost Fifties were indeed mysterious and intimidating. She knocked on the heavy wooden door on the first floor of the third section.

"Come in!"

She pushed open the door but remained standing in the small hall with her back to the only one other room in this hallway. A narrow staircase led up to three more floors—like one of those old brownstones with two apartments on each floor. She thought they seemed much cooler and more private than the dormitory type barracks everywhere else.

"May I come in?"

"Yes, ma'am." Cadet Calloway stood up. He was wearing his white cadet PT shirt tucked into his gray sweatpants.

"No need for any of that...spring leave and all..." She also wore the standard PT uniform: gray sweatshirt over gray sweatpants.

"Yes, ma'am." He pulled out his roommate's chair. "Would you like to sit down?"

She didn't get a good look at him while they were walking the Area, but now that she sat facing him, she felt her face redden. He was handsome, very handsome. He looked to her like he came from Alaska or Hawaii or the Samoan Islands. His eyes tilted up slightly at the ends and his skin was the color of a chocolate milk shake. Jan thought he looked delicious. She tried to keep cool, to act cool, to at least look cool. "So why are you doing this?"

"My little sister was raped. I would love to kill the bastard who did it, but we may never know who it was." He looked down at his Etonic sneakers.

"When did it happen?"

"Last year. When she visited me at the prep school. She didn't tell me until almost three months later."

"I'm so sorry."

"Thanks." Silence hung between them as Jan tried to think of something to say. Calloway spoke first. "So when I heard what happened last year, what you and Cadet McCarron did, well, you guys are my heroes."

Jan fidgeted in the chair. *What do I say to that? Thank you?* "We certainly didn't plan that outcome," she said finally.

"Oh, I know. But you took one bastard off the streets. And for that, I am very glad. I'd like to kill the one that raped my sister."

Jan could feel goose bumps rising on her arms. *Is this guy for real?* "Okay, so why don't you kill Mullenbehr? He raped Cadet Wan, right?"

"Yeah, that's true. If Cadet Wan was my sister, I probably would." He looked around his room. "Obviously, I can't go around killing people. But I figured I could do something. That's why I went to Mullenbehr with my tape recorder on."

"And you're going to give me this tape, right?"

"Yes. Do I have your word that you will get it to the newspaper guy?"

"Yes." Jan stood up. "Now I need to get back to my room." *Before my knees give out.*

Calloway walked to his desk, opened his bottom drawer and lifted his gray lockbox onto his desk. He entered the combination to his lock, opened the metal box and pulled out a TDK cassette tape.

"How did you hide the tape recorder? It's pretty big isn't it?"

"I taped it to my leg and wore dress gray. You'll hear my trousers swishing on the tape."

"Ingenious." Jan reached out to take the evidence from Calloway. But he held onto it with both hands. "Are you reconsidering?"

"Um...I'm just wondering. Can I trust you with this?"

"Who else would you trust?" She tried not to look in his golden brown eyes.

"I'm not sure. But I don't even know you and I'm giving you this damning piece of evidence."

She stared at him hoping he couldn't read her mind. She was thinking how much she wanted to kiss him.

She took a step toward him. "I guess you're just going to have to trust me."

She felt her neck turn red and more goose bumps erupting on her back. *Remain calm, cool and connected.*

She saw his Adam's apple rise and fall in his throat and wondered if he was thinking similar thoughts.

She reached her right hand forward, brushing it against his left hand before latching onto the cassette tape. "I promise to take good care of it."

His cheek twitched slightly. Jan realized he was struggling too and she didn't think it had to do with the evidence.

He released the cassette and let her take it. She held it up slightly and said, "You're doing the right thing."

"I hope so." Jan saw his Adam's apple bobble again. "Ma, am," he added, as if reminding them both of something.

"I have a tape recording of Mullenbehr—admitting to raping Cadet Wan," Jan whispered into the receiver inside the small pay phone booth on her hallway.

"No shit?"

"No shit. You have to come up here ASAP, while everyone is gone." Jan knew Drew never planned to visit West Point again. Being kicked out of the United States Military Academy, no matter how unjustly, never leaves your bones. It lives with you like a constant, dull ache or a minor cough you just can't shake. "The plebes don't know you and they ignore me, so the timing is perfect."

"Well, I suppose I can visit this once, since it's in support of the mission."

"Yes, and you get the added benefit of seeing me."

Walking the Area was forbidden on Sundays, being a "day of rest" and all. Instead, Jan sat four hours of room confinement, which counted for two walking hours. Then she walked four more hours on Monday. She had only ten hours left to walk.

Drew arrived Monday night, just before Taps. She escorted him to her room and closed the door. When Taps played, Jan stood near her door and waited for the CQ's nightly bed check. In a few minutes, the plebe knocked twice.

"I'm here," she shouted without opening the door.

"Okay, goodnight, ma'am."

"Goodnight."

With only the light of her desk lamp, Drew and Jan sat huddled together, listening with the volume down to the tape recording Calloway had given her. It was damning. It would, indeed, provide the evidence to nail Mullenbehr.

Jan pulled out another tape recorder and made a copy of the original. "Just in case something happens to that one," she said.

"Good idea."

She put the copy in her lockbox and gave the original to Drew. "Now, in honor and tribute of your esteemed visit, let's celebrate!"

She opened her bottom desk drawer and pulled out two Diet Cokes, placing them on the desk. She walked to her closet, bending down to the floor. Between the bottom drawer and the wall was a small space, hidden behind the wood trim. She pulled the molding away, reached into the dark hole and pulled out a plastic saline solution bottle.

She walked to the sink cabinet, collected two small, clear glasses and returned to her desk. She poured the liquid from the saline bottle to fill one-third of each glass. Then she added the Coke, filling to the rim.

"Cheers!" She handed Drew one of the glasses.

He took a sip, screwed up his face and said, "Damn, you still make the best vodka Cokes."

They spent the night laughing and reminiscing on Jan's bed until 0300 hours, when they finally fell asleep under her Gray Girl.

Jan walked four hours each on Tuesday and Wednesday. She watched silently as the plebes enjoyed their freedom—tasting what their lives would be like when they finished their first year. Even though they'd still be restricted to certain areas, even though they'd still have to wear a uniform everywhere, even though they'd continue to be under enormous pressure both academically and physically, and even though they'd be engulfed in a crucible of unrealistic standards, everything after plebe year still feels like a cake walk. As she finished her 118th hour of walking the Area, she suddenly seemed to realize the point of plebe year.

It's so that nothing else you do will ever seem impossible...

KNOCK, KNOCK!

"Yes, I'm here."

"Okay, ma'am, goodnight."

"Night." Jan kept writing in her journal after the CQ bed check on Wednesday night. She felt somewhat excited about finishing up the last two hours the next day. Then she would be free to go on spring leave. However, with no car, no friends in the area and only a few days left, it didn't mean she would have any fun.

Tap, tap, tap.

Jan looked up, wondering who would be knocking after Taps. She slid off her bed, dropped her journal and pen and walked to her door.

It was Cadet Calloway.

"May I come in?" he whispered.

Jan stuck her head into the hallway, checking to see if anyone had been watching. When she saw the coast was clear, she motioned for him to enter and closed the door behind him.

"What are you doing here?" she asked.

"I'm having second thoughts about the tape. Do you still have it?"

Jan sat down on the edge of her bed. "No, I already passed it on."

"Shit." He sat down on Esther's bed opposite Jan. "I should have edited it first so that my name isn't audible. I didn't think about it until today, but once my name gets out..."

Jan bit her bottom lip. "Yeah, you'll be like those frogs that gave birth out of their mouths..."

"Huh?"

"Gastric-brooding frogs—the last one died in captivity this year." She paused. "Don't you read *The New York Times*?"

Calloway's quizzical look transformed to a half smile, then a chuckle, then full-on laughter.

"Shhhhhh!" Jan jumped on him, putting her hand over his mouth. "Not so loud, or you'll wake the neighbors," she whispered, while laughing herself.

His lips were suddenly on hers and they locked themselves in passionate kissing. They fell back onto her rack, still kissing like new lovers. For the first time in forever, Jan wished she didn't have a boyfriend. She wished she could be someone who could look the other way when it came to cheating. She wished she could keep going with Calloway, who seemed to be enjoying himself as well.

But that just wasn't Jan. She knew she had to put a stop to it. She could never look Rivers in the eyes again and she could never look at herself in the mirror, if she allowed this to continue.

"Calloway!" she whisper shouted his last name. "You have to leave."

"C'mon, Jan..."

It pissed her off that he knew her first name when she didn't even know his. "Now!" She ordered.

He got up, straightened his PT uniform and walked to the door.

"Wait!" She jumped up, opened the door and peered into the hallway. "Now," she whispered, indicating the coast was clear.

She closed the door behind him, wishing she could be more callous.

TWENTY-NINE

"In my dreams I hear again the crash of guns, the rattle of musketry, the strange, mournful mutter of the battlefield."
(Douglas MacArthur, USMA Class of 1903)

March 31, 1983
1645 hours

Jan returned from her last Area tour on Thursday to find Violet lying on Esther's bed, her travel bag on top of Esther's footlocker. "Why're you back?"

"Joey's spending the rest of the week with his friends, so I just returned a little early." She seemed satisfied with this arrangement.

"Why didn't you go somewhere with your friends?"

"Well, I don't exactly have any friends, except you, Pamela and Kristi."

"Oh, okay." Jan didn't want to say what she was thinking, which was that they didn't exactly consider Violet their friend.

"I have to stay with you until my roommates return. Company policy."

The Corps-wide policy required all women cadets to share a room with at least one other woman at all times. Cadet doors did not have locks and this measure was supposed to ensure their safety. Jan didn't want to room with a beanhead all week, so she never mentioned anything about being alone in her room, and she was happy when no one bothered to enforce the rule.

"Sure thing. Glad to have the company," Jan lied. She would have been glad to have Pamela or Kristi's company. Violet, on the other hand, always seemed needy. She went from being skinny one month to being kind of chunky the next. She fought endlessly with Joey and sported new bruises every week. "I just finished my Area tours, so maybe we can go to Ike Hall tonight for a couple beers."

"No thanks, Jan. I really need to catch up on my sleep."

See what I mean?

Peter is lying facedown in a pool of blood. His legs are splayed at awkward angles.

NO! NO! NO!

She finally reaches her brother and turns him over. He is still breathing through the stab wounds to his chest. She can see his breath going in and out of each puncture.

Dammit! Hang on, Peter. Help is coming. Please, hold on.

Why? He asks her. Why?

I don't know. I don't know. I thought...I thought...

She wants to say: I thought you were someone else. I thought you were trying to kill me.

Somehow, it doesn't make sense anymore.

Peter's face suddenly transforms. He's no longer her brother. He is no longer human. His face becomes alien, creature-like. His hands metamorphose into claws, he grows a tail, the holes in his body become eyes.

She stands up and shrieks. What are you? What have you become?

She looks around and sees nothing. Nothing. Dark grayness enshrouds her. She doesn't know which way to run.

She can't see her hands or her feet. Everything is covered in thick ash.

She runs anyway. Anywhere. She runs and runs and runs. It doesn't matter where. She only knows she has to get out of the choking fog.

Jan woke up with her pillow covering her head. She glanced over at Violet sleeping on Esther's rack and wondered why she allowed Joey to treat her like a slave. Here was a nice looking, well-educated young woman, surrounded by a sea of eligible men who would treat her like a queen if they could.

Yet she tethers her reins to an ass...

Jan would never understand how some women—smart women—could be so stupid when it came to men.

Jan arose, went to the latrine and brushed her teeth. She changed into the running uniform—gray sweatpants, gray sweatshirt and Etonic sneakers—then headed out of the barracks for a morning run along the Hudson River.

It was one of those cool, crisp, glorious mornings at West Point, when everything seems to glisten under the rising sun. The statues, the cannons, the iron fences, even the Gregorian brick townhomes, called Colonel's Row, were all lined up, dress-right-dress. *Present and accounted for.* She ran up the hill to the Cadet Chapel—the queen of all the buildings on Post—and noticed for the first time, the splendor of the Gothic Revival architecture. Before, it had always seemed menacing and dreary, but on this morning, with the sun casting its early rays on the massive wooden doors, it somehow seemed inviting—comforting even.

Will I ever feel comfortable here?

She pondered the question while running all the way to Michie Stadium and Lusk Reservoir.

Sir, there are 78 million gallons when the water is flowing over the spillway.

This statement, memorized during plebe year, just popped into her head. Then the answer to her first question came: *Probably not.*

She looped around the stadium and began the descent toward her barracks, deciding to take the stairway near the chapel. It led a hundred or so steps down to the back of the mess hall, where she turned right toward New South. As she approached the final ramp to her building, she saw Myrna Watkins walking up the opposite ramp from Thayer Road.

What's she doing back this early?

It was Friday morning and the upperclasses didn't have to be back until Sunday night.

Jan decided she didn't care why Myrna was back early and certainly didn't want to stop and chit-chat about anything with the woman who caused her to miss spring leave with her boyfriend. She pretended she didn't see Myrna and continued running up the ramp, reaching the barracks door first and entering without saying a word.

She walked into her room and found a note on her desk.

Hey, babe! I couldn't wait until Sunday! Come upstairs and we'll plan our weekend getaway!

Love,

Rivers

"What? Is everyone coming back early?" Jan asked the rhetorical question out loud.

"Why, who else is back?" Violet sat up rather enthusiastically for someone who appeared to have been sleeping when Jan entered.

"Oh, I just saw my ex-roommate, Myrna."

"Why's she back?" Violet asked.

"I didn't stop to ask her," Jan said while heading toward the door. "She's not someone I care to talk to—ever."

Jan ran upstairs to Rivers' room and flung open the door.

"Ah, good thing I wasn't naked." He walked toward her.

"So what if you were?" She closed the gap. They hugged and kissed passionately. Even though Public Display of Affection (PDA) was not allowed anywhere on Post, they practically had the place to themselves and since it was still early on Friday morning, they took the risk. The beanheads probably would not report two upperclassmen making out.

"Daytona Beach was okay, but I just kept wishing you were there."

Jan suddenly felt stabbed by guilt. Almost as quickly she convinced herself that Rivers must have had at least one one-night stand.

"Oh? Not enough hot babes in bikinis for you?"

"There were plenty of them. But...not one of them was you."

Shit. Did he have to say that?

She smiled. "So you're saying you missed me?" She kissed him again, hard.

"Yes, ma'am!"

Jan requested leave for the rest of Friday through Sunday. Having finished her walking tours, even the TAC could not deny her those three days. While she packed her bag for the weekend, she told Violet she would need to room with one of the plebes for the next two nights.

"I thought you said Myrna was back," Violet said.

"Oh, yeah, I guess you can room with her if you want," Jan replied while assembling her toiletries.

"It's better than rooming with a beanhead." Violet began gathering her things as well.

"Okay, well, whatever suits you. I'll see you Sunday!" Jan hurriedly exited her room. Only Later would she regret not having lingered a bit longer.

THIRTY

Under certain circumstances, urgent circumstances, desperate circumstances, profanity provides a relief denied even to prayer.
(Mark Twain)

April 3, 1983
0500 hours

"Jesus," he whispered.

"Oh my God!" she replied.

They stood in silence for several minutes while staring down into the ravine at the red car. Jan wondered how long it would take for the wheels to stop spinning.

"We should get help," he said.

"Yes, let's go," she replied shaking.

Jan and Rivers sat on the trunk of his car. Waiting. After the accident, they frantically drove a mile or so to the first house they saw. Jan pounded on the door, yelling, "We're West Point cadets—there's been a crash! Please call for help!"

The elderly couple hesitated slightly before agreeing to call the police while Jan waited on the front stoop. Rivers stayed in the car until she returned. They drove back to the scenic overlook to flag down the help that was to come.

Yet they knew that no amount of help would help. Whoever was in that car had died, they were sure of that.

"It's Joey's car, isn't it?" Jan asked.

"Yeah, pretty sure," Rivers sighed.

"Did you see who was driving?"

"No, I only saw taillights as it sailed over…."

"I think I caught a glimpse…"

"Did you see a passenger?"

"I think," Jan said, feeling certain she saw two people in the front seat. "But I can't be sure."

They spent several hours answering questions, filling out forms and going over and over the sequence of events. The ambulances arrived but the victims could not be reached. A rescue squad had to be called in to rappel down the cliff with gurneys in tow. They would lift the injured to the roadway where the ambulances could take them to the hospital. That was the hope, anyway.

The police allowed Jan and Rivers to return to West Point just as the rescue teams began the delicate operation. Jan was glad to leave before the gurneys came back up the cliff. She didn't want to see who would be on them.

They returned to the barracks at fifteen hundred hours, having agreed not to mention anything to anyone. In case they were wrong, in case it was some other red Camaro, in case the car had been stolen—whatever. They hoped against hope the car was not Joey's and that Violet would be found in her room, safe and sound.

Jan dropped her bags in her room and followed Rivers to his room, where they left his things. They both walked next door to Kristi, Pamela and Violet's room, looking at each other once more before knocking.

"C'm in."

Pamela sat at her desk, painting her fingernails with clear nail polish. "Hey, Pamela." Jan tried to sound chirpy.

Pamela looked up. "Hey, how was your getaway?"

"It was nice," Rivers said, "a little too short, maybe."

"Yeah, well, you guys will have a few weeks together after graduation. That'll be fun, right?"

"Yeah." Jan looked at Rivers. "Yeah, that'll be great." She realized her plans for a relaxing summer break may be put on hold indefinitely. "Hey, have you seen Joey and Vy?"

"Yeah, apparently he came back yesterday and they drove into the city, I think." Jan knew what Pamela meant—New York City.

"Ah, did they say when they'd be back?" Jan asked.

"They already came back."

Thank God, they're safe.

Pamela continued, "They got back last night and promptly got in another fight."

"So they're both still here, right?" Jan asked. *Please say yes, please say yes.*

"Well, Vy was so upset that she took off again in his car. Boy, oh boy, he must've done something really bad this time."

"Where'd she go?"

"I don't know but Kristi went with her, just to make sure she'd be all right."

"WHAT? KRISTI'S IN JOEY'S CAR?" Jan screamed.

"Geez, Jan, calm down." Pamela put the nail polish away. "Joey gave them permission to use it...."

"NO! GOD! NO! NOT KRISTI!" Jan cried.

Pamela stood up. "What's wrong? What happened? Did something happen?"

Rivers quickly shut the door. "Shhhh!" He turned to face them. "Both of you...sit down."

Jan and Pamela sat down on opposite beds, facing each other.

"What is it?" Pamela asked. "Tell me!"

"Oh God, Pamela, we think we saw Joey's car go off a cliff on Storm King Highway," Jan whispered.

"NO!" Pamela shouted, covering her mouth with one hand.

Rivers jumped in again. "SHHHH! You guys need to keep it down...we don't want to alarm anyone. And we can't be sure whose car it was."

"Did they say anything about where they were going?" Jan asked Pamela.

"No. Vy just wanted to get the hell away from here and Kristi offered to go with her," Pamela said. "She thought Vy shouldn't be alone."

"Jesus, please let them be safe," Jan whispered.

"What should we do, Jan?" Pamela asked.

"We wait," Rivers said. "There's nothing we can do to change the situation. Either they're okay or they're not."

That seemed as promising as anything.

They waited in agony. Jan jumped every time she heard voices in the hallway, hoping one would be Kristi's or Violet's. Even though the women weren't hungry, Rivers ran to Tony's, the pizza place in the middle of Central Area, and brought back a pepperoni and mushroom. He was the only one to touch it. Nothing seemed to curb his appetite.

At 1930 hours, when all cadets were required to be back on Post, Jan ran to the latrine and began throwing up. Pamela followed her and rubbed her back while Jan sobbed over the white porcelain vessel.

"Kissy's gone! My best friend is gone! She's never coming back!" Jan cried between regurgitations.

Pamela, also in shock, tried to soothe Jan. "It's okay, Jan, it's gonna be okay..."

"No!" Jan felt spittle dripping from her mouth. "It's never going to be okay. Never...again..."

"Shhh...Jan, maybe it's not Joey's car...maybe..." Pamela continued to rub Jan's back, trying to rationalize that Kristi would be okay, somehow.

"What the hell are you two crying about?"

Pamela turned her head just as Jan rotated hers. Kristi stood at the entrance to the toilet stall with a slice of pizza in one hand and a Diet Coke in the other.

The crouched women pounced, knocking Kristi into the lockers behind her. The Coke and pizza went flying as they pinned their friend in bear hugs.

"Hey, what's the matter with you guys? That was the last slice..."

"Kristi! You're alive!" Jan exclaimed and hugged her again.

"Yeah, I think so, now let go of me," she said.

"We thought you were dead," Pamela said.

"Now why would you ever think something like that?"

At 2100 hours, Joey Lishiski came to their room as Pamela, Kristi and Jan huddled on Violet's bed.

"Is she back yet?" he asked.

"No, we haven't seen her," Pamela said.

"What exactly did she tell you, Kristi?" Joey asked as he walked to the middle of the room.

"I told you already—she said she had something to do and that she had to do it alone. She dropped me off at the Bear Mountain Inn and told me to call someone for a ride."

He seemed agitated. "Did you even ask her where she was going?"

"Yeah, I asked her," Kristi said, "but she said it didn't involve me."

"So you just let her drive off in my car?" he asked in an accusatory tone.

"No, Joey, *you* let her drive off in your car, remember?" Kristi was good at this.

Joey stormed out of the room without responding.

The trio bent their heads together. In silence, they waited and prayed, each in their own way, for a miracle.

Violet didn't return that night or the next morning. At lunch formation, word spread that there had been an accident involving a cadet on Storm King Highway. Jan kept checking in with Rivers, Kristi and Pamela, who didn't seem to know any more than she did. At dinner formation, Jan looked over to Company H-1, noting that Joey Lishiski was absent.

John Heggenbach stood behind the table commander's chair and stared down at Jan. She stood behind the third chair from the end wishing the Wizard of Oz voice would announce "TAKE SEATS" from the poop deck.

"What do you know about your friend, Violet Carpetta, in H-1?" John asked.

"Excuse me?"

"Violet Carpetta is AWOL. Where is she?"

"How would I know, John?"

"She's your classmate and roommate of your best friends."

"Well, they don't know much more than the rest of us."

"TAKE SEATS!" The mess hall erupted in the noise of the dinner meal—chairs sliding, utensils clacking, plates banging, plebes shouting and upperclassmen laughing.

Jan thought the sounds of dinner had never felt so comforting.

"ATTENTION TO ORDERS!" After several administrative and athletic announcements, the Oz-like voice said, "With deepest regret, we report that Cadet Violet Carpetta, Company H-1, has died. More information will be forthcoming. Let us bow our heads in a moment of silence for Cadet Carpetta and her family."

All activity stopped and the mess hall fell strangely silent. Jan bowed her head.

Please help her family. Please help. Please.

After a two-minute pause, the voice made one last comment. "Amen."

"Drew, it's me." Jan said into the black handset of the hallway pay phone booth.

"Hey, girl, what's new?"

"Violet is dead."

"WHAT?"

"She drove Joey's car off a cliff."

"Oh, no! Are you shitting me?"

"I wish I was. Listen, has the next installment gone to press yet?"

"No, the final draft is due tomorrow. Why?"

"I have more information. You've got to include it in this next article."

"Okay, Jan. Tell me what you know."

THIRTY-ONE

The press is like the peculiar uncle you keep in the attic - just one of those unfortunate things.
(G. Gordon Liddy)

April 8, 1983
0700 hours

What's Happening to Women at West Point?
(Part 3)
By Steve Calibrio, staff writer

Since my last installment in this series, there have been a few alarming developments. Most notably is the death of a woman cadet, apparently by suicide, this past weekend. I will address that situation later in this article.

First, I want to pick up where I left off last time with the young woman who was raped by a high-ranking officer's son and a fellow cadet. She was effectively forced to resign. I am currently in possession of a tape recording where the alleged rapist clearly admits to sexually assaulting this young woman. The conversation between the two cadet men, whose names are also clearly stated, is a damning piece of evidence against the young man whose father holds a prestigious position at West Point.

By the time this article goes to print, I will have transferred this tape recording to a special panel that is investigating the unusually high number of women who have left the academy this year. When they hear what is on this tape, I think this case will have to be reopened and the young man in question must be held accountable for his actions.

For the record, however, I have made a transcript of the entire recording. Here is an excerpt:

Cadet A: Sir, Cadet A reporting to Cadet B to make a statement.

Cadet B: What is it, A?

Cadet A: Sir, I saw you leaving Cadet C's room that night she claims she was raped.

Cadet B: Yeah, so?

Cadet A: Sir, I also saw you had scratches and bite marks on your face and hands.

Cadet B: (chuckling) Okay, anything else you want to say, Cadet A?

Cadet A: Yes, sir. I didn't think anything of it then, but since I read the article, I think she was telling the truth. I think you raped Cadet C.

Cadet B: Is that so, A? Well, well, well...

Cadet A: And I feel it's my duty to report what I saw...so I'm just telling you first, before I go to anyone else.

Cadet B: Go right ahead, beanhead, tell whoever the hell you want. You think anyone's going to give a shit? It's old news, pal, even if you say something now, it won't matter. I stand by my claim—it was consensual, we just got a little rough. So go ahead, spout off all you want about what you supposedly saw—it makes no difference to me. (He lowers his voice) I got what I wanted and there's not a damn thing you or anyone else can do about it.

Cadet A: You mean you did rape her?

Cadet B: Shit, yeah, she had it coming. But go ahead, friend, go snitch on me. Let's see how that works out for you. You might just regret getting involved, beanhead.

The conversation continues with the brave plebe suggesting that Cadet B turn himself in to save his dignity and to do the right thing. Cadet B then seems to realize he has admitted too much to Cadet A and tries to backpedal on his earlier comments. He denies having raped Cadet C, after all. They merely had rough sex, he insists. Cadet A leaves as Cadet B begins shouting and threatening to use the Honor Code against Cadet A.

I believe this is an authentic recording that reveals Cadet B's guilt and exonerates the young woman who was forced to resign. I hope, as do many others, that the investigating panel will do the right thing with this piece of evidence.

Now, back to the woman cadet who allegedly committed suicide by driving off a cliff on Storm King Highway last weekend. My highly reliable source at West Point has provided a bit more information.

The young woman, let's call her Mary, was a yearling (sophomore) cadet. She was dating a firstie (senior) cadet, we'll call him Ben.

Mary and Ben have been together all year. It has been widely known that Ben treated Mary badly, he openly yelled at her and called her names. Mary seemed to sport new bruises weekly.

Additionally, while all cadet women feel pressure to be thin, Mary's weight seemed to fluctuate more than most. She would at times appear chunky, and then in a matter of weeks, her weight would shift to the point where she looked almost too thin. Mary was known to throw up a lot, claiming she had a "weak stomach."

Last week, the upperclass cadets left for spring leave. Mary and Ben had planned a trip together, but Mary returned on Thursday, claiming that Ben had decided to spend the rest of spring leave with his friends. She returned to West Point, even though she wasn't required back until Sunday evening. Mary roomed with women in another company, as per policy that women cadets never stay in a room alone.

According to my source, Ben returned to Post on Saturday morning. He and Mary had another huge fight, which was partially witnessed by Mary's roommates. For reasons that are still unclear, Ben allowed Mary to take his car Saturday night. One of Mary's roommates, worried about her emotional wellbeing, decided to go with her.

The two friends drove around for some time and stopped at a diner in Poughkeepsie, just north of West Point. Sometime after four a.m., Mary deposited her roommate at Bear Mountain Inn, saying she needed to do something alone. The roommate offered to wait, to drive, to call someone, to do anything that might help Mary's mental state. Mary simply said she had to do this thing alone, and that the friend should call for a ride back to West Point. The roommate felt that Mary seemed calm and self-controlled. She had no reason to think Mary would be a danger to herself or others.

Sometime in the early morning hours on Sunday, Mary drove Ben's car off the cliff, killing herself.

Now, when the dust settles and the investigation is completed, we may discover that Mary had psychological issues. She may have been bulimic and emotionally fragile. Perhaps she wasn't suited for a place as difficult and stringent as the United States Military Academy.

But when all else is said and done concerning Mary's tragic choice, there is still one very clear and resounding fact: She was an abused woman. And it appears that the man who abused her is going to be commissioned as a second lieutenant in the US Army in May of this year.

C'mon folks. We've got to do better for our women in the military.

THIRTY-TWO

"Pray, and let God worry."
(Martin Luther)

April 23, 1983
1400 hours

Jan looked up from her pew. The soaring stone arches met in curved triangles far above her head. *One, two, three, four...*she began counting the flags hanging below the rows of stained glass windows lining each side of long, narrow cathedral. They resembled a formation, each one dressed right and covered down. The organ began to play a sad but beautiful tune. Jan remembered that the West Point Chapel boasts the largest pipe organ in the world, with 23,511 individual pipes...another one of many things they had to memorize plebe year.

She sat next to Kristi, Pamela and Rivers in the third row from the chancel area. The rest of Company H-1 filled that pew and the next four or five behind them. Violet's family took up the first two rows. Everyone else in Third Battalion, First Regiment sat somewhere in the chapel, except for Joey Lishiski.

He was brought before a Regimental Disciplinary Hearing immediately after the last article following Violet's death. He flatly denied ever abusing Violet. However, Kristi, Pamela, Jan and Rick testified about their observations of Joey and Violet's relationship. When Jan and Rick revealed what they heard that night in the dayroom, well, that pretty much sealed the case. Bruises, witnesses, continuous fighting, and the on-and-off relationship—all spelled doom for Mr. Lishiski. Yet even faced with all that evidence, Joey continued to deny ever lifting a finger toward Violet.

The Regimental Disciplinary Board decided they had more than enough to label him an abuser, but his flat denials of abusing Violet only made it worse for him. Had he just admitted to the abuse, they might have required therapy or some remediation program whereby he could be rehabilitated, along with a healthy dose of walking tours. He might still have been able to graduate.

Given that he continued to deny the accusations, however, they felt an Honor Board was more appropriate. The Honor Board got underway only two days after *The New York Times* article. Jan, Pamela, Kristi and Rick recounted everything again, just as they had told the Regimental Disciplinary Board. Joey Lishiski was found guilty of violating the Honor Code and expelled from USMA. He was to report to Fort Bragg in June to serve two years in the Army as a private first class, as repayment for his West Point education.

Good riddance.

Jan smiled at the only positive thing to come out of Violet's death. *At least we took care of that for you, Vy. I hope you're at peace now.*

The chaplain began to speak.

"Have you never heard? Have you never understood? The LORD is the everlasting God, the Creator of all the earth. He never grows weak or weary. No one can measure the depths of His understanding. He gives power to the weak and strength to the powerless. Even youths will become weak and tired, and young men will fall in exhaustion. But those who trust in the

LORD will find new strength. They will soar high on wings like eagles. They will run and not grow weary. They will walk and not faint.

My friends, today we bear witness to our faith and remember the power of the resurrection, which causes us to rejoice, knowing that our sister, Violet Carpetta, now resides in the Kingdom of Heaven.

Yet there is also great sorrow to have lost one so young, so vibrant, so full of life—one who was dearly loved by all who knew her—and one whose life was cut short by the complexities of this life, which cannot be fully understood or explained. We live with this mystery everyday. We will never know why Violet took her own life, but we know with absolute certainty that she is a child of God, who loves us much more than we even know—much more than we love each other, much more than we love ourselves. So in that certainty of God's love, we proclaim the power of the resurrection, which Christ gave His life to secure, so that we might all live eternally with God.

Friends, we do not need to worry about Violet anymore. She is completely free—free from the worries and the disappointments of this life, free from the heartaches and sorrows in her heart, free from the body that restricted her to this earth—she will never be lonely, fearful or sad again. She is shining in the eternal light of heaven, she soars on wings like eagles, she runs and does not grow weary, she walks and is not faint.

No, it is not for Violet that we have gathered here today. It is for family, friends and all those whose faith is challenged by her passing. How do we go on? How do we fill the void or make something good out of the emptiness that is now present in her absence?

This is the real work of grief. This is our task at hand. We must take all that Violet's life can teach us and use it to inspire, to help, to grow, to be the very best people we can be so that Violet's life will be even greater than it was. She will have touched even more people that she already has. Her life will continue to give life—if we allow it to inform us and to transform us.

This is, after all, the beauty and the mystery of resurrection. It is an eternal truth, whereby we live forever with God after this life, AND we can be renewed and reborn, again and again, during this life.

It's all a matter of listening and hearing, of watching and seeing, of breathing and hoping, of praying and believing, of loving and learning.

Hold on, friends. Although the sorrow comes, and even stays a while, remember that God always wins. God always has the last word. God always loves us, abides with us and takes us home at the last. We have already won.

Violet just got there before us."

Jan didn't understand most of what the chaplain said. Yet she felt the speech contained beauty, wisdom and truth. She longed to know what he seemed to know, she longed to have what he had—some kind of peace—a presence that seemed solid, steady, unruffled.

What is that?

After the service, Jan walked back to the barracks with Rivers. They only had a few more weeks before graduation.

Then what happens?

They hadn't talked about the future. She knew at least two of her classmates were quitting to marry their firstie boyfriends at the end of May. Marriage was not even on Jan's radar. Still, she wondered if they would continue to be a couple after this year. Rivers was going to be stationed in Georgia for six months before going to a unit somewhere in the world. She still had two more years at West Point, which normally might not be a problem.

Except for Rick, and now, Calloway.

She didn't picture herself with more than one boyfriend at a time...but she wasn't sure she wanted to be attached to one who was so far away when two other viable options were close by.

Gawd, I'm awful.

Love? No, Jan wasn't in love. She didn't have any idea what that even meant. She only knew that she wouldn't give her life for Rivers. Therefore, in her mind, she couldn't possibly be in love with him.

But he was still the best (and only the second) boyfriend she ever had. Didn't that count for something?

I am going to miss him.

Now that she thought about it, Rivers hadn't mentioned anything more permanent either. He didn't seem to want the long-term relationship any more than she did.

Maybe he's hoping to find something better. I can't blame him.

Jan convinced herself that neither of them loved the other and both of them wanted out after he graduated.

There, that settles it.

"One down, one to go." She didn't realize she'd said it aloud.

"What do you mean?" Rivers asked.

"I mean, well, Joey's gone. Now we just need Mullenbehr to get booted."

"That's far less likely, since his dad is the commandant."

"Yeah, but with the tape recording and all?"

"I heard it was a fake."

"What?"

"That's what everyone's saying."

"It's not a fake!"

"How do you know, Jan?"

"I just know. He's guilty, that's all there is to it."

"Well, don't get involved, please...you don't have a dog in that hunt."

I kinda do.

Jan decided not to say anything more.

THIRTY-THREE

"It's good to beat your head against the wall—it's sooooo good when you stop!"
(Letter from dad, Cornelius F. Ives, 1983)

May 7, 1983
1200 hours

By the end of April, the secretary of the Army's panel investigating the unusually high number of women cadets leaving West Point made its list of recommendations to the superintendent of the United States Military Academy. In addition, they reviewed the circumstances surrounding each woman's case and advised that at least three women be offered reinstatement. One of those was Cadet Wan.

They also required the tape recording be sent to a special Department of the Army lab, where it was tested against another recording of Cadet Mullenbehr's voice. If the voice on the tape was confirmed to be Cadet Mullenbehr, he would be expelled immediately and court-martialed for the crime of rape.

The lab results determined that the quality of the recording obstructed an accurate assessment of the voice authentication. A swishing sound, probably from the recording cadet's trousers, inhibited the verification process. However, with what could be heard on the tape, they deemed it unlikely to be a match with Cadet Mullenbehr's voice. In other words, even if the quality of the tape was good enough to get an accurate reading, they did not think the voices matched.

Mullenbehr was neither expelled nor charged with anything.

Cadet Wan chose not to return.

Jan made her way over to the Lost Fifties. She knocked softly on Calloway's door.

"C'm in."

She opened the door, saw he was alone at his desk, closed the door and walked toward him. "Was the tape real?"

"Yes, of course, it was."

She sighed. She believed him. She sat down on his bed. "I guess we should have known they'd figure out a way to get him out of it."

"Yeah, and now I'm a marked man."

"I know. But there is one thing you have in your favor."

"What's that?"

"You need to let Mullenbehr know that if anything happens to you, you've arranged for a copy of the tape to be brought to an independent authenticator. That new assessment will then be brought to *The New York Times*."

"Jan, I didn't make a copy."

"I did."

He stood up and kissed her.

"I know you have a boyfriend, but I don't mind if you want to hang out with me every so often," he said after a second or third kiss.

"That's very kind of you," she said, "but I should be going."

"Okay, I understand."

She turned and walked to the door.

"Hey, Jan?"

"Yeah?"

"Ut sementem feceris ita metes."

She stood there for a long moment, trying to remember where she had heard that. Then it dawned on her. "You did that?"

"Yup. Mullenbehr will get what's coming to him."

"We thought it was meant as a threat to us."

"Well, it works both ways...you sow evil, evil comes back to get you. You sow good, well, that's what comes back too."

"I like it. Is it from Shakespeare or something?"

"Ha, ha...something like that."

"I guess I'll see you around next year," she said.

"Yeah, and your pesky boyfriend will be gone then, too. Lucky me."

"Ha, ha...something like that."

She kept smiling all the way back to New South.

THIRTY-FOUR

"There is no sinner like a young saint."
(Aphra Behn)

May 11, 1983
1900 hours

In the second week of May, Jan and her classmates were given their summer assignments. They were required to participate in one of several "schools": Airborne, Air Assault, Jungle Training, Survival-Evasion-Resistance-Escape (SERE) or Northern Warfare Training; and one Command Troop Leader Training (CTLT), acting as a second lieutenant in an actual unit.

Being petrified of heights, Jan chose Northern Warfare, Jungle and SERE in that order. But when the orders came down, she had been assigned to Airborne School, where she would have to make five parachute jumps. She would report to Fort Benning, Georgia three weeks before the start of next year's classes.

As for CTLT, her orders were to a basic training unit at Fort Dix where she would lead new recruits in PT, boot shining, room cleaning and drill for six weeks.

Jan ran up to Pamela and Kristi's room. "Well, what did you get?" she asked as she pushed open the door.

"I'm Airborne." Pamela got her first choice.

"I'm going to the jungle," Kristi said disappointedly. She had also wanted Airborne.

"Hey, can we swap orders? I'm happy to deal with snakes and insects instead of jumping out of perfectly good airplanes." Jan hoped this might be possible.

"No, Jan, they won't allow that. Kristi already asked to change with someone and the TAC said absolutely not."

"Damn," both Kristi and Jan said at once.

"How the hell am I ever going to jump out of an airplane?" Jan sank on Kristi's bed.

"Well, first you will have to jump from the two-hundred-and-fifty-foot towers," Pamela said.

"Oh God, no."

"And because we're in the last summer session, we cannot be recycled, like those in the earlier sessions," Pamela added.

Airborne school was notorious for its physical standards—if you didn't keep in the runs or do the minimum amount of pushups or sit-ups, you could be "recycled" to the next session. If you didn't qualify during Tower week or Jump week, you could try again with the next group. But being in the last summer session meant there were no do-overs. No second chances.

Everyone at West Point knew when someone failed Airborne School. Even with a legitimate reason, like a broken leg, Airborne "rejects" were always marked as failures. Especially women. Everyone knew which women did not earn their wings, and that cloud hung over them their entire time at West Point.

Jan made up her mind. If she didn't make it through Airborne School successfully, then she would not come back to USMA. She would resign at the end of the summer, before the first day of classes cow year, when the five-year requirement to serve in the Army went into effect.

Jan and Rivers scaled back their nocturnal activities. Being so close to graduation, neither she nor he wanted to get caught doing anything that might result in a huge slug and/or prevent him from graduating with his class. However, they still went off Post legally whenever they could. They snatched time together in pieces, both knowing these would be the last for a while. Maybe forever.

Jan continued to see Rick at Team Handball and formations. They remained cordial but distant. Jan could not imagine ever seeing him again as a boyfriend type.

Just not in the cards.

Jan decided to ask John for her book back on the day before graduation, just after they finished recognizing the plebes.

He's had it long enough.

She knocked twice on his door.

"C'm in."

She swung open the door. "John, I'd like my book back, please."

"What book?" He stared at her.

She stared back. "You know which one."

"Oh, yes, that one." He smiled and got up to unlock his trunk. He reached down and picked up the book, still with its fake *To Kill a Mockingbird* cover on it. "Here ya go."

She walked to him and took it from his outstretched hand.

"It was a very interesting read," he said.

"I'm glad you liked it."

"Yeah, it was enlightening, you could say."

"I'm sure it was," she replied.

"Do you always read that kind of...literature?"

"Oh, only when I'm bored..."

"I see. Well, thank you for letting me borrow it."

"Well, it's not like I had a choice."

"You could have come for it a long time ago...I would have given it back."

"I was afraid to ask for it," she admitted.

"I can understand why...but it is your book."

"Did you share it with anyone else?"

"God no. That's highly sensitive information."

"It certainly is. Thank you for keeping it between us."

"Of course, did you think I wouldn't?"

"I didn't know what you were doing with it...I just hoped you'd be discrete."

"Discretion is the better part of valor, Jan."

"Thanks again." She turned to leave.

"No, THANK YOU." He smiled at her.

THIRTY-FIVE

"How easy it is to judge rightly after one sees what evil comes from judging wrongly."
(Elizabeth Gaskell)

May 24, 1983
1600 hours

Jan shoved five pairs of fatigues, eight pairs of green socks, ten OD green t-shirts and both pairs of black combat boots into her green duffle bag. She had already moved her two footlockers, filled with most of her cadet uniforms, to the basement locker room. West Point uniforms would not be needed at Fort Dix or Airborne school. All the other stuff—hangers, books, blankets, pillows, etc.—went into one closet where it would stay until she returned in late August. She left out only her toiletries and dress gray to be worn at graduation the next day.

Jan glanced around the room. Esther had already packed her things and was out somewhere with Adam. Leslie had also vacated Post with the tennis team to attend a two-week training camp. Jan would see Leslie again at Airborne school.

Just like old times.

She couldn't help thinking it might be a repeat of Beast, where Leslie would do everything exceptionally well and Jan would just try to survive.

Well, it has been almost two years since then...I'm much stronger and smarter now. I'll be fine.

She continued to make positive statements to herself as she glanced around the room. She felt like she was forgetting something...what else was there to do?

Oh, right. "I almost forgot," she said aloud.

She bent down at the corner between her closet and the wall, pulling back the molding strip and reaching into the hiding spot. She felt for the plastic saline bottle. When she didn't readily feel it, she stuck her hand farther into the opening. But it wasn't the saline bottle that her hand touched first—it was a leather-bound book. She pulled it out.

Hmmmm. She reached back into the small hole, bringing out the plastic bottle. She brought it over to the sink, took off the cap and began draining its contents. Once it was empty, she rinsed the bottle several times before throwing it in the trash.

She brought the small notebook to her bed and sat down. She opened the front cover.

Jan,

Please read this diary to the end. I wish you all the best,

Violet

Jan could hardly believe it. Did Violet really leave this diary for Jan to find? Why? What could she possibly want Jan to know? She sat on her rack, back to the wall, her feet hanging off the edge of the bed. She began reading the dead woman's journal.

August 29, 1982

I think I'm in love! I can't believe it! It's not supposed to be like this—it can't be. But here I am, in love for the first time. I feel like I will explode with joy on one hand—and burn in hell on the other. I want to tell everyone—and no one. I feel such pride—and shame. How can this be?

Of course, I can't tell anyone. If anyone knew about us, well, anyway...we know what we have to do. We have to be discreet. Very discreet.

Why would Violet feel she had to hide her relationship with Joey?

September 12, 1982

I had the best weekend! We made love about ten times! It was sooooooo great! I can't stop smiling and thinking about it. I wish I could tell everyone how happy I am.

Yet this can't be right. There has to be something wrong with me. How can I feel both joy and shame at the same time?

On top of everything, Joey Lishiski has asked me to the Ring Weekend festivities. It's best if I go...go along with...whatever. It's best for everyone.

What the hell was Violet up to? Who else was she seeing?

September 19, 1982

I just made myself throw up again. It's probably not the best way to keep the weight off, but I don't want to be the chubby girl I was last summer. That was disgusting.

October 3, 1982

We haven't been able to see each other very much. It's just too risky. We did manage to sneak in one "quickie," which was marvelous.

In the meantime, I'm getting more involved with Joey. He's a nice guy. He's good to me. I feel a little bad about pretending with him, but we both think it's best to keep the relationship going.

And of course, I still feel incredibly guilty. This is so wrong, in so many ways.

What was she doing? Was she seeing a plebe? An officer?

October 12, 1982

I wish I could throw up. I don't know what to do. My love…hit me. Hard. No one's ever done that before. I am sick, sick with worry.

Maybe this is my punishment for doing evil. Maybe I deserve to be hit, over and over, for what I've done.

But all I can do is eat. Which is making me feel even worse.

Jan gasped. *OH MY GOD.*

October 31, 1982

It happened at least twice more. I don't know what to think, I don't know what to feel. I say, "I love you," I show how much I love…so why does my love keep doing this to me?

Maybe God is trying to show me that this is wrong…that I need to get out. I know it's sinful—and I deserve the beatings. But I can't seem to leave my love. How can I be so screwed up?

Joey and I are going deeper. Maybe that's why…even though my love wants me to keep playing the role, maybe my acting is TOO good. Maybe that's why it's happening so much.

FUCK! Joey was NOT the one beating her???

December 10, 1982

I didn't write anything for a long time because I needed to focus on getting my weight back where it needs to be. I went home for Thanksgiving and even though I ate WAY too much, I was able to purge most of it. I feel like I'm finally getting back on track.

I also needed a break from everything. But then I agreed to meet my love for the last two days of Thanksgiving leave. It went well for the first day. I felt so great. I was thin again and I was with my love.

And then the hitting started again.

I can't stand it anymore. I'm in love. But I cannot go on like this. I know I'm sinning against God and I must suffer for my transgressions. I am ready to repent and change my evil ways.

Joey has no idea...he loves me. He was so sweet to me when I returned to Post. He missed me and we snuck out to make love. He is always so tender and kind to me.

Jan jumped off the bed, ran to her trashcan and threw up on top of the saline solution bottle.

Jan 15, 1983

Okay, that's it. We're done. I can't keep this up. I still love...but I can't do it anymore.

I have Joey. We have a good relationship. I am only going to focus on him from now on. I'm going to let him have every bit of me. I'm not going to hold anything back from him. He deserves the best I can give.

Jan 27, 1983

I allowed Joey to make a tape of us together. I hope to watch it and see if it will make me feel like a "normal" person.

I am so confused. Throwing up seems to be the only thing that makes me feel better.

Feb 6, 1983

Dammit! I should have known I would be drawn back in. What the hell am I going to do??

March 12, 1983

I'm fat again, and I fear I will never be able to stay thin. On top of that, I know I'm going to hell.

But I can't help it. I can't seem to stop overeating and I can't seem to stay away from the one who hurts me the most. I'm so weak.

We have a plan for spring break. I'm going to go with Joey for the first half. Then I will come back here and we will have a few days together.

It will be wonderful.

It will be awful.

I can't wait.

I dread it.

Jan rinsed out her mouth. *It must be a married man!*

April 2, 1983

I hate myself. I hate what I've become. Today I saw myself for who I truly am. I am a fat, sick, sinner with no hope of redemption.

I also saw "my love" for what it is—a sham and a reckless waste of time and energy. I have been such a fool.

I have sinned against God and I fear I will never be able to change.

I hate myself more than ever.

What have I done? What have I done?

I am beyond saving.

April 2, 1983

Jan,

I'm leaving this diary for you. Please do what you think is best with it. Obviously, I have tried to protect the identity of my lover. But I see no need anymore.

Myrna Watkins is an abusive, manipulative, violent bitch. I loved her, I really did. But I cannot live with what I have done. I hate myself. I hate what I have become.

I have become like Myrna. I have ruined everything—for myself, for my family and for Joey. I have been so wrong—so wicked. I deserve to burn in hell for my sins. I cannot go on living like this.

I'm sorry. Please tell my family I love them.

I love Joey, too. Please tell him for me.

Vy

Jan dropped the leather-bound book on the bed and ran to the latrine. She rushed to a stall and threw up again. After regurgitating the contents of her stomach, she rolled onto the floor next to the commode. She stayed there for a long time, weeping.

Oh God, I've condemned an innocent man!

Jan remained lying the floor of the latrine praying to her Banker God—one who would not likely help her now. Still, she had to ask.

God, help me.

Please, help me.

I need your help, please.

I need you.

Please.

She finally arose and rinsed her face in the sink, looking in the mirror. "What are you going to do now, Gray Girl?" she asked aloud to her reflection.

"You will find a way," the face in the mirror replied.

Jan took a deep breath, opened the latrine door and walked back to her room.

She was certain she had left the diary on the bed. She bent down and looked underneath the rack.

Nothing.

She lifted the mattress off the metal frame.

Nada.

She looked in the trashcan, under the vomit and in all her desk drawers. She even looked in Leslie and Esther's drawers.

Nope.

She opened all the closets and the laundry bins—she even rechecked the liquor cabinet in the wall.

It was gone.

"Jan, Jan," she heard someone calling her from outside the window of her room.

She ran to the sill and pushed the double hung window further down from the top. She climbed up onto the sill and looked out to New South Area. There were several cadets walking around with their duffel bags—all preparing to vacate as soon as graduation ended the next day.

"Jan, over here," she heard the voice shout.

Perched on her knees, Jan looked to the right. Myrna Watkins was standing next to a brand new red car parked on the ramp between New South barracks and the cadet store building.

She waved something in her right hand while grasping the door handle with her left. She opened the door and sat down in the driver's seat. Jan listened as Myrna started the car and revved the engine. Then she drove down the ramp and onto Thayer Road.

Jan slid down from the windowsill. It took another few seconds before she realized, with renewed revulsion and nausea, that Myrna had waved Violet's leather-bound journal.

Postscript

In my time at West Point, a few cadets had eating disorders, were abused by their lovers and were closeted gays and lesbians. These were the days before "Don't ask, don't tell." The Army policy then was: "Don't be gay." I suspect the same was (is) true at many colleges across America.

As with *Gray Girl*, the events in this book are not true, yet they could be considered authentic. I've embellished and/or totally made up incidents that might have occurred or could have occurred. I've also compressed various personalities into a single character. Authentic, yes; true, no.

If you enjoyed this book, I hope you will rate it favorably on Amazon.com.
You can contact me directly at:
GrayGirl2013@gmail.com
You can also follow the Gray Girl series (hint: more to come) at:
https://www.facebook.com/GrayGirl2013

About the Author

Susan I. Spieth graduated from West Point and served five years in the Army before attending Seminary. She earned a Master of Divinity degree and is ordained in the United Methodist Church. She served five churches as Pastor/Associate Pastor for seventeen years. Susan and her husband have two children and live in Seattle, WA.

Area Bird is her second novel in the *Gray Girl* series.

Made in the USA
Lexington, KY
02 March 2015